STEVIE SM[illegible]

was born in Hull in 190[illegible] her parents and sister to A[illegible]ress now immortalised in [illegible]ore stage play, *Stevie*, and its [illegible]red Glenda Jackson. Here [illegible]her parents' death living wi[illegible]t'.

Born Florence Marga[illegible] Bolognue the jockey, she went to [illegible] Green High School and the North London Collegiate School for Girls and worked until retirement as private secretary to Sir George Newnes and Sir Neville Pearson, the magazine publisher. She first attempted to publish her poems in 1935 but was told to 'go away and write a novel'. *Novel On Yellow Paper* (1936), was the result. This and her first volume of poems, *A Good Time Was Had By All* (1937), established her reputation as a unique poetic talent and she published seven more collections, many of them illustrated by her own drawings. An accomplished and very popular reciter of her verse, both on radio and at poetry readings, she won the Cholmondeley Award for Poetry and, in 1969, the Queen's Gold Medal for Poetry. She wrote only two more novels – *Over The Frontier* (1938) and *The Holiday* (1949).

Stevie Smith died in 1971. In 1975 her *Collected Poems* were published, a selected edition appearing in 1978. Virago publishes her three novels together with her hitherto uncollected works – stories, essays, poems, letters and a radio play – in a volume entitled *Me Again*.

VIRAGO
MODERN
CLASSIC

NUMBER
19

Over The Frontier

by

STEVIE SMITH

WITH AN INTRODUCTION
by
JANET WATTS

Published by VIRAGO PRESS Limited 1980
20–23 Mandela Street, Camden Town, London NW1 0HQ

Reprinted 1983, 1985, 1989

First published by Jonathan Cape Ltd 1938

British Library Cataloguing in Publication Data

Smith, Stevie
Over the frontier
I. Title
823'.912[F] PR6037.M43

ISBN 0-86068-130-0

Printed in Great Britain by
Cox & Wyman Ltd., Reading, Berks

INTRODUCTION

This is a novel about war. It comes from a surprising hand. Its author was an idiosyncratic woman and a highly original poet, but – as she was the first to admit – no soldier. 'Pompey very very bad soldier,' she mused, as her jovial doctor injected her arm. 'There I knew it, and never had it occurred to me in reason that I should at any time be a soldier either good or bad', she wrote in this book published a year before the outbreak of the Second World War.

Stevie Smith lived all her life in the same tranquil London suburb; she worked for thirty years in a publisher's office unshattered by shells. The nearest she got to the theatres of battle was in the holidays she enjoyed some years before their European locations came under the pressure of war. (She took what she called the 'first last train' out of Berlin after one such sojourn in 1931.)

Yet in this book the unmistakably Stevie-centred Pompey Casmilus, whom we have already met in its predecessor *Novel on Yellow Paper*, finds herself thrust into a tough and terrifying life of military espionage: nocturnal reconnaissance rides on horseback; daring acrobatics for eavesdropping and observation; homicide in the course of duty; and the achievement of a position of massive human responsibility in the confidence of certain unpleasant characters who are stage-managing a European war.

This extraordinary adventure story succeeds the novel's first half, whose subject-matter is as dear and familiar as home to lovers of Stevie Smith's poetry and earlier prose. It is the continued saga of Pompey Casmilus's life and mind: Pompey at home with her beloved aunt in Bottle Green; Pompey in the last agonies of rupture in her friendship with Freddy; Pompey in London art galleries, peculiar parties, office longeurs; at gossipy lunches and in country weekends.

Pompey, in delicate health and vulnerable post-Freddy *tristesse*, takes off on a recuperative holiday with her friend Josephine to a Schloss somewhere on the Baltic coast. Under its therapeutic and nanny-strict régime she sails, swims, converses, and gets bored to death. Whereupon the inner and outward ramblings of this familiar Pompey suddenly flow into the dramatic excursions of a new one, in an adventure story that has something of the quality of a dream. Perhaps it really is a dream. We know that Pompey is a great and vivid dreamer. 'Often when I am dreaming asleep I look at myself in a mirror, and I think. Why I might be real it's so good it's just like you could touch it.' (*Novel on Yellow Paper*). And the dream-like happenings of this book's second half indeed fulfil a real dream in the first.

Still safe in her dull, irritating, ordinary world on the day she arrives at the Schloss, Pompey dreams that she is with Freddy, her lover whom she does not love, and she is in uniform. He notices it, she denies it: she shouts and swears by Christ's blood and cross that she is not in uniform, she has no commission, she is under no orders. But some weeks later, the dream returns, and soon after that, it becomes reality.

On a night ride desperate with troubled thoughts, Pompey breaks the mask of stupidity of Tom Satterthwaite, the British intelligence officer; some days later she crosses with him the frontier that divides the worlds of peace and war. 'Oh war war is all my thought. And suddenly I am very alert and not dreaming now asleep at all.' Pompey dresses reluctantly to make that journey, and sees in the firelight the mirrored reflection of clothes that are not her riding habit. 'The flames on the hearth shoot up and their savage wild light is reflected at my collar, is held reflected and thrown back with a light that is more savage, but completely savage, with the flick of a savage quick laughter the light is tossed back again from the stars upon my collar and the buckle at my waist.

'I am in uniform.'

The stunning image is at the heart of this book. It curiously recurs in another book published in this year by another woman whose gently bred but ruthlessly investigative mind penetrated deeper into the mysteries of war than many a bemedalled general's. Within the delicately-wrought polemic of *Three Guineas* Virginia Woolf revealed 'the figure of a man. . . .

'His eyes are glazed; his eyes glare. His body, which is braced in an unnatural position, is tightly cased in a uniform. Upon the breast of that uniform are sewn several medals and other mystic symbols. His hand is upon a sword . . . And behind him lie ruined houses and dead bodies – men, women and children.'

And now Pompey is in uniform: the gentle, humane, remorselessly analytical Pompey. Pompey, that strong spirit on the other side of the frontier from the rising mania of Germany, has in all her awareness been drawn across it. 'I grind my teeth to think of Germany and her infection of arrogance and weakness and cruelty that . . . has set on foot this abominable war, has brought us all to this pass, and me to a hatred that is not without guilt, is not, is not a pure flame of altruism; ah, hatred is never this, is always rather to make use of this grand altruistic feeling, to bring to a head in ourselves all that there is in us of hatred and fury. . . .'

Pompey-Stevie was ever remarkable in self-knowledge, in admitting her community with ignoble humanity. She put it in a poem –

> Do not despair of man, and do not scold him.
> Who are you that you should so lightly hold him?
> Are you not also a man, and in your heart
> Are there not warlike thoughts and fear and smart?
> Are you not also afraid and in fear cruel . . .

In prose, Pompey has always monitored the blackest specks in her soul. In *Novel on Yellow Paper* there was something – not anti-semitism, no – but something that felt elation at a Jewish party – 'Hurrah to be a goy!' – and that later felt the tweak of a link between that and the horrors in Germany, 'as if that thought alone might swell the mass of cruelty working up against them'. Now in the Schloss Tom Satterthwaite craftily touches Pompey on the same nerve over the tinkling teacups, and casts her into 'despair for the racial hatred that is running in me in a sudden swift current, in a swift tide of hatred . . . Do we not always hate the persecuted?'

Pompey is us: we are Pompey. And Pompey is in uniform. Not

just when she crosses over the frontier, but throughout this book, she explores and experiences the world of war. Long before she leaves her sideline, she 'frets at every bit . . . longing to be off': full of that 'nervous irritability that has in it the pulse of our time. For we have in us the pulse of history and our times have been upon the rack of war. And are, and are . . .'

Stevie Smith lived all her life on the safe side of the frontier. Yet with that extraordinarily unlimited consciousness that vitalises all her writing, she was also the victim, prophet and antenna of everything that happened in the world beyond it. The gentle and non-combatant Stevie was also Pompey, her pride and ambition, fury and hatred, 'rising like a high wind' as she gallops into the war, fatigue forgotten in its excitement. 'I laugh and laugh with delight . . . and thank the God of War to be rid of the tea-cups and tattle . . .' She knows, and shows, what the pacifist Vera Brittain recognised as 'this glamour, this magic, this incomparable keying up of the spirit in a time of mortal conflict' (*Testament of Youth*).

Yet at the last Pompey is herself still: nobody's fool. Not the war god's; not even her own. 'How apt I was for this deceit, how splendid a material, that recognising the deceit must take commission under it . . . I may say I was shanghaied into this adventure, forced into a uniform I intuitively hated. But if there had been nothing of me in it . . . should I not now be playing, in perhaps some boredom, but safely and sanely enough, with those who seem to me now beyond the frontier of a separate life?'

The sideline observer who becomes the committed warrior cannot escape a final, cold, and certain awareness of the truth beyond the deceptions on both sides of the frontier. Pompey saw the cruelty and the 'dotty idealismus' that 'upon this side of the frontier marches with the enemy'; against it her hatred and fury rose, and she believed 'we shall win . . . we are right'. But at the peak of her military career she discovers a more appalling reality. Finally, coldly, and certainly, she perceives the identity of the warring spirits, the ineluctable baseness of all power and privilege, personal and national, on either side of the frontier. 'I have been mistaken.' The heart and the knowledge of Pompey-Stevie were indeed no soldier's.

Janet Watts, 1979

He certainly is the funny man; why he certainly has a funny angle on life, why certainly there is this very cynical and malicious laughter that goes echoing round this elegant picture-gallery. Among all the picture-galleries of London this picture-gallery has all of the laughter that is not just simple happy fun, why not that at all, no, in this elegant gallery in the best part of the picture-gallery parts of London, why for instance there is *Ballyhoo* and the *Cahiers d'Art* and Aristotle opposite to this gallery and is not this all very high-class and slap-up?

And by-and-by if you go round the corner there is that flight of stairs which has Venus at the top of it, and once there was a man that had got funny in his head with drinking a lot of Schnaps, and by-and-by he got up those steps and was stroking this Venus in a very deep-going and affectionate manner, he certainly had a strong natural affection for Venus and what more like than he should go to stroking this classical plasteret to show how he was feeling this very deep-going affection that was so right and natural and at the same time so simply free and outpouring? But by-and-by the man that stood there in uniform, he was a very formal character, very hardened in the emotional arteries, well, see if he must not go and give him a great push that sent him falling falling down that flight of stairs where at bottom he fell a victim to a horrible whore.

This is the truth of Jack's tale, that I told you before, that he told me a few days ago, and thinking quietly of this tale I came through the portals of this elegant picture-gallery. My mind was full of art and I had a nostalgie to be looking at these high-up and elevating canvases and there was especially the one that is called 'Haute École'.

Now this one I will tell you about. So. There is this very classical animal, this horse, that has a vivid plastique tail and his front leg is raised up to do the high step. His colour is a light and beautiful brown colour that hardly serves to cover the canvas, so ethereal and noble is this animal and his nostrils are spread wide. Very elegant indeed and high-born is this horse with his wide open eyes his wide-spread nostrils his sleek coat and his wide wide eyes that have that look in them that is a warning to the people that know about horses like me. But oh how splendid is this high and elegant horse that has in him and in his limpid and ferocious eye all the sense of that 'Hohe Schule' and all of the centuries of traditional comportment. On this horse's back sits a man that is perhaps not so entirely classique as this noble animal, because I am thinking now there is something about this man that is a little fin de siècle, for instance he is long and slim but though this is how the long lines of his body lie there is also at the same time about him that feeling of plumpness that is a little feminine and his face is so plump as the faces of some of the slim full faced pouting degenerate people that you have in the drawings of Beardsley. So. He has no hair on his head at all he is absolutely bald and his head has a pink plump covering of soft flesh and his lips are pursed and pouting and his eyes beneath puffed eyelids are looking downwards. Very sly very supercilious are the lineaments of this man's face. His long slim body is clad in black, it is a sort of '*smoking*' he is wearing. He has no hat and there is no hat in the picture, so if he falls if he falls well shall I say that he will not fall a victim to a horrible whore, but if that malicious and indignant horse if he prances sideways and makes suddenly to shy then off will come the man, pitching forward on to the hard floor of the riding school and with nothing between his plump pink hairless head and the hard hard floor it will go hard with him I guess it will be all up with that hatless rider.

Oh the colour in this canvas how lovely it is how beautiful how lightly touched in with what skill and what wisdom so to leave the canvas bare with such precision with such significance to express so much to be so entirely necessary inevitable so never to be thought of until it is done and then how else could it ever have been thought of for one moment to be done.

Oh there is a very great genius in this picture and oh now how greatly I am wishing to possess it. So I say to the man who is in this elegant picture-gallery, he is a little short of breath, I ask him to tell me how much is this beautiful picture for which I have so great a tendre and this acquisitive feeling that possess it I must. Oh it is nothing says the short-of-breath man it is nothing just forty guineas that is what it is and is. O heart of pain and empty purse how come to forty guineas that is so much of what I have not got. So he says: *Very witty this painter is he not?* Oh yes, he certainly is the funny man. But oh I have a tendre for this horse and rider so I must look at the other pictures and forget and forget. I know this artist very well I know his black-and-white work, but never before have I seen his paintings and never before should I have thought for one moment that he could have projected this thought of this ferocious and captive animal and his degenerate rider. Oh hush now hush and remember to be reasonable and to look here and there, and to judge and to discriminate and not to make a fuss-up about this ha-ha horse that never can be yours. So. There are a lot of still lifes, no they are not anything so good, no I will say now that I am not partial to Mr. Grosz's still lifes. Very often have they been painted by painters before to be hung in galleries, they are, this is what I should say, the still lifes of to-day in the current mood, that is to say there is that seashell Gefühl about them and the superficial incongruity of selection that is not contributing anything that is fresh but is only just superficially incongruous like I mean like a bad Bernard Shaw. So. But then there are some very cynical and malicious black-and-whites and colour-washes that take me right off again right off my heart of pride to say No he is not so good. But there is quickly now I will tell you there is 'The Assignation', that is certainly very funny: the girlie is rather fat and has on those funny 1928 clothes very short in the skirt and very high in the hat and so looking like a bolster that has short fat legs that go bulging over the cheap thin shoes. There is a sugar daddy that is looking at the girlie he is thinking he is thinking Well is she worth it, chaps, is she worth this famous RM 20 note that is at the present moment safe in my elegant pigskin pochette? And on the whole you guess the answer will be, I will knock her down to RM 10. I said I'll knock her down to RM 10. I said RM 10 is my limit. I said. There is also number 79 that is called 'Girl Guides' that I think will certainly not have at all a great appeal for Lady Baden-Powell. There are these girl guides, there are these two girls sitting on the ground and the curve of their plump thighs comes out of the too tight elastic band of their directoire knickers. So. One is playing a mouth-organ, very arch is the look in the eyes of this one, and the other sits and sings and sings with her mouth wide open and her little teeth, too small too small for the English taste, so very much too small too sharp and too white. There is something vicious about these sharp small white teeth that is offensive to the English taste that has always a fundamental but often unarticulated and even unrecognized preference for teeth that are long and strong and looking rather yellow. No. 77 is 'On the Beach'. This made me laugh and there I stood laughing and laughing, with the man who is perhaps only rather short of breath standing beside me. 'On the Beach' goes like this. There is a beachbasket like they have at Swinemünde and all along the flat coastline of the Ost-See bathing resorts. In this beachbasket is sitting an old girl who is really so extremely ugly and so extremely amorous that it is something to give you a good laugh. Three cheers for the old girl in the beachbasket that is peering round the corner of the beachbasket that is looking this way. She has a sharp pointed nose and little eager pig eyes and a hat raked on her head that has wisps of hay-hair rioting out from underneath this so-smart toque. And what is she looking at what is she looking at oh? Well, chaps, she is sitting looking at a fine nordic specimen that is full to the brim with masculine buck and that has such a cast in his eye that. Oh Strandkorb shield me from the strange man with the cast in his eye. But no, she must have her love and affection and also he is holding a camera. Oh scintillating vanity of unsatisfied desire, oh what a pity it is that the beach is so jam full of girls and boys and bathing attendants and ice-cream vendors that never for one moment can they be alone, oh certainly it is punk for those two that never can they be alone to obtain *eine seelische Entlassung* and a nice holiday snap to set on the mantelshelf beside the artificial roses. And looking and laughing and thinking of all this my thoughts turn again to a darker memorial I have of Georg Grosz that is this dark memorial that is called A Post-War Museum where all of the ignobility and shameful pain of war suffering is set down with the precision of genius and the bitterness of a complete experience, oh here in this portfolio are such things as our security cannot conceive, cannot bear for one moment to contemplate. People say, Why, such things cannot be true, no it is a neurosis, why this George Grosz he is just a war neurotic, it is sad but he should certainly be shut up and prevented, why it is not at all a good thing that he should be let run round to infect with his neurosis his defeatism his anti-sozialismus the healthy unthinking happiness of our sheltered infant adults.

But oh the tearing seering suffering of Germany after the war, the disintegration and diminution the backward journeying the fear the cringing corroding terror of poverty and hopelessness, The Old Men of 1922, the old broken shamefully broken body of the shattered soldier drawn up lifted up crucified upon his crutches lifted up above the old-young child, and over it all and undertoning it all is shame and loss and flight into darkness. Oh no no no, for us there is now not this Post-War Museum at all it is not in our experience we do not wish to understand or to think about it at all, it is for us somebody else's cup of tea that we do not even say: May it pass from us, that we do not have anything at all to do with. So a victory has given us at least this that we do not have to taste this cup of tea. No. For us there is this funny-ha-ha Georg Grosz that has his witty drawings and paintings in this elegant picture-gallery I was telling you. So Georg Grosz is out of Germany now he has made an escape to America and I am glad that he has done so. So now he can forget, or with the will not to remember he can have his American citizenship, and he can be still perhaps a little bitter and have his cynical laughter go echoing round the picture-galleries of London and New York, but it is only, Very funny, very clever, is it not? So he has created this laughing and ferocious horse, this so classical animal with his wide wide eyes that are so full of passion and integrity, oh this high-stepping horse that is so high up and arrogant, how very pure is his colouring how plastic and precise the draughtsmanship this picture that is forty guineas, and what is there still to say about the rider? He is perhaps rather a nigger in the woodpile, there is perhaps something a little enigmatical about this rider, after all what is he doing? I think he is doing this, with great application and concentration this is what he is doing, he is forgetting to remember the shame and dishonour the power of the cruelty the high soaring flight of that earlier éclaircissement, that was that pale éclair dans une nuit profonde, that rakehell of a beam of light that went showing up the very sad bones of that earlier situation, this he is very actively forgetting and instead he will think of the easy generous light-running laughter of the English and Americans, and he is thinking of that American nationality that shall come dropping down dropping like a curtain to shut off from him for ever that sad sad situation, that already perhaps he is a little ashamed to have seen once and for all time so top to bottom, so round and about and within, so in its flesh and bones and skeleton its sinews nerves and muscles, to the very last outposts of the black heart of despair of the situation.

Even manly hearts may swell
At the moment of farewell . . .

How true the poet's sentiment, benign, how *noble*. And if the manly heart, what of the heart feminine, may not that swell and fail and tear and burst for the sadness of a mismanaged love-situation, that is so much at this moment the situation between my departed Freddy and myself.

Yes, no. What of the heart of Pompey that lay down to die with the tigress Flo, to decline upon her paws, to give up a life that was so hateful. See my last book, Reader, where it says about Pompey and Flo.

And coming out of this picture-gallery I must think of my own situation that is so heavy upon me. And I think: I will be so sad and, Nothing shall save me. For me there shall be no curtain, no curtain at all, to come dropping dropping down, to be in this way *my America*, *my New-found-land*, my sanctuary, my salvation and escape. And I think, I will keep my eyes to a low place of funeral, and no woman and no man, indeed no man ever again, shall scour the heart of Pompey that is now numb and ripe for death.

And enjoying and turning upon myself in my great disturbance à l'égard de cet ineffable Freddy, I am thinking, Now my whole life is about to end, and everything is penultimate, and all these days are penultimate, and so now what is left of my life shall be a voyage autour de ma chambre.

Oh Pompey, think and count the flowers on your wallpaper, and remember to be sad, and remember and remember.

So now of course I was getting rather ill. And the doctor said, You must take some Glaxo-Glucose D, and you must take This, and with your meals you must take This, and at night-time you must take this sleeping tablet, and when you wake up in the morning you must take another.

So I was thinking, It is funny to take a sleeping tablet in the morning when I have immediately to go to my office, to be this grand private secretary to Sir Phoebus Ullwater Baronet, and also I was thinking, There will not be time to take all these medicines. So it was getting rather funny. For if I was not swallowing pills that were so large you might hardly come to swallowing them, then it was a liquid medicine that I was drinking, or these sleeping tablets that were not so large, but dissolved very quickly to give to the drink-water a flavour that was very funny-peculiar indeed, very deathlike. So my life although penultimate became rather a burden. These days, Reader, were sad, and a great exasperation and irritation, but hardly to be borne.

But now my so-good and kind friends, who had not at this time read my book, they become very staunch and true, and I was every Friday catching a train somewhere. It was, one weekend it was Anna and Ian who have a nice house in Essex, but it is rather cold, and another weekend it was my dear friend Harriet, and another weekend it was Mary of Oxford, and another weekend it was William.

So at last the weekend came when I was to go down and see chère Josephine. So I packed my case, and very distraught and wild in the head, I go down to see Josephine in her little town by the sea.

How hot that train was I can remember. How it was like it was an oven. But everybody at the same time was complaining of draughts. And particularly hot and foetid was it in the restaurant car, that never had a window open, but was smelling of human beings and biscuit crumbs that have been scattered a long time ago, and now even the mice will not have them, No, thank you very kindly, we are passing the biscuit crumbs this time.

So at the station Josephine met me in the car, so almost at once we come to Josephine's bungalow that lies a long way back from the road. And there with a cocktail ready for miserable Pompey is kind Uncle Ivor.

So I am telling you about this weekend because now it was that the great idea came to Josephine that I should go with her and with the beautiful little girl Reine to Schloss Tilssen. There is nowhere on earth (I thought then) I would rather go than to Schloss Tilssen, so already after dinner, thinking about this splendid idea of Josephine's that we should all go together to Tilssen-beyond-Pillau, I began to feel lighter in my heart, and thinking hopeful-absurd thoughts about this grand destination I said: Yes certainly that was a good thought of Josephine's, and she is a darling, and I will go with her, and it shall be for us both an amusement and an escape.

So when the time came to go to bed I kissed goodnight to Uncle Ivor, who is now looking very old and frail. But I did not kiss goodnight to Josephine, because presently I knew Josephine would come to my room.

And presently when I had had my bath I went into my bedroom where the fire was burning brightly in the open fireplace and the logs falling softly together as the fire burned them up to fine ash, and presently Josephine came in to sit on the hearthrug and talk.

But only she should have had a great deal of long hair to brush and brush while she was talking, so that would have been 1910 and la vie heureuse before the war came to put another thought into the feminine head, that only before then had to think of love and the trials and pleasures that make up the temperate hairbrushing confidences of that period.

But now it is all very different from that, and there is a great burden of stress and strain, and only with Josephine sitting on the hearthrug brushing her hair in the firelit room can I recapture the outward semblance of that earlier reminiscence.

But Josephine's voice is going on and on, and it is very pleasant to lie here in bed and listen and not listen. And to think and to think, that peace comes dropping slowly, slowly. So slowly you would not notice. Why it certainly is not pouring. Why certainly you will not need an umbrella. Peace is dropping slowly, very slowly, it will hardly leave an outward rime on your coat of magic mail that wraps you round from sorrow.

'What are you taking, Pompey? What is in those tablets that you are swallowing?'

'Why these are the tablets that clever doctor gave me. I take them to sleep. They are just two tablets that I take every night.'

(Sweet Josephine is getting a little pop-eyed at this. What alluring vision of drug-fiend friend to be rescued with nobility of patience from a toil.)

'But Pompey, you want to be very careful. Now what is in these tablets?'

'Well what is in them is what is in them is luminol and chloroform and valerian.'

That is enough to keep a tiger quiet. You must think that this tiger that had taken this luminol and chloroform and valerian could only just so much as stretch his claws, stretch his claws every twenty-four hours and turn over again to sleep and be at peace in his head.

The next day we took the car into the New Forest and walked there in the sunshine, and in the afternoon I went down alone to the seashore and sat there for a long time. It was warm and damp in the late afternoon. And I sat on the shingle and watched the sun setting over towards Swanage. It was very blood red and shone a golden light on to the wide sea, that was the colour of a bright warm rich dark paint, that shines, that is neither yellow nor green, but between the two colours, very tawny, very shining. It is like the paint in Harriet's flat.

The shingle was shifted high up by the Christmas

tides, and stripped brushwood lay round about, and the cliffs behind were bright red clay, and very wet and dangerous to walk upon. There had been a landslide, and there lay all the rust and rubble of the red clay, and the damp turf still sticking to it, right down and across the beach to the white surf that curded up the steep shingle bank.

I had on my feet a large pair of nanny's wellingtons that came right up above my knees. And I ran down the steep shingle bank into the Christmas sea that came hissing and curding round my ankles, covering them over and splashing up to my knees, and whirling and scooping back again and out to sea, to leave the green seaweed climbing upon my feet.

Here I was enjoying myself very much, with the wind blowing in my face from the open sea. And so the time passed quickly, and it was time to remember that it was time to go home to Josephine and to run into Josephine's bedroom and say: 'Wake up, Josephine, it is tea-time.' And Uncle Ivor must come too, and Josephine from her hot-water bottle, and Reine from the nursery fire. And old Mrs. Job, that is Josephine's cookie, brings the crumpets and the cake and the teapot. And now it is suddenly all very animated, and we are talking and laughing a lot. And Uncle Ivor is telling a great many animated stories in French, and these animated stories are getting very extremely bawdy. But

Reine, who is five, listens, and her blue eyes are very dark and wide open, and she says: 'Auntie Pompey, I am having French lessons now.' So that is rather a rift in the lute of the animation of Uncle Ivor.

But when Josephine is taking Reine to bed, Uncle Ivor rallies and tells me tales of the Malay Peninsula, where, as a young man, he was stationed for a time. But these tales, they are funny, but they are not perhaps funny enough and that is a fault. There is nothing worse than the not perhaps quite funny enough. For this, Reader, is what the young man said to me when I sent him a poem. And then I felt, There is certainly nothing worse than to be not funny enough. Indeed it is better to be serious. And I thought, In future I will just write little delicate and sad pieces that are full of unshed tears, and at the same time *noble*, and not only thinking of the funeral paths, and of the dead man lying in the grave beneath, or of the church that stands out, a darker shadow against the dark shadows of the storm-swept midnight moonless sky, but that is waiting for the chords that will come, that are coming now, in Beethoven's funeral sonata, to bear up with them on their mighty wings the spirits of the redeemed.

But what is Uncle Ivor saying, saying sitting there in the firelight, twisting and turning in his thin old hand the stem of the glass that so worthily bears Uncle Ivor's special cocktail? (This is a very potent drink, rather like Kirschwasser with a dash of absinthe, the recipe for which he will not give me, the recipe for which he has culled in the far far East, remote in space and time, the Far East of Shanghai, Hongkong, Malaya, Somerset Maugham and Mr. Wu.)

But what is he saying, what is this kind Uncle Ivor saying? Well then, he is telling me how he has ridden a polo pony. No, it is ridden a polo pony and led two unridden polo ponies, along the corridor of the mezzanine floor of the Hotel Lord Mounsel at, well where is it, I forget. And I am wondering what I can say when the pause comes to cap this famous exploit. And he is telling me the bawdy story, 'J'ai touché le bouton à . . .' that is at the same time, perhaps I have got it wrong, not Uncle Ivor's story at all, but the story of the bawdy friend that he told me to pass the time of day. And pray what can I say, when the pause comes, as it must, however it comes, to cap this famous bawdy tale? Then: 'Come quickly, mama, cookie is buying a policeman' and, or, and 'Look what the black protestants have done to Father O'Reilly' that is Freddy's story. Ah how nervously irritating are the imminences of these pauses in the flow of the raconteur. Ah it is extremely unquiet this sort of a talkie, that has these pauses coming on. It is a spiritual irritation, yes, it is very disturbing to me. Oh how bored I am when people will tell these funny stories, with the expectation of a something that is to come from you when the pause comes that is to be filled.

This was the last night that I spent at Josephine's. So in the late evening she came again to my hearth-rug to brush her hair and to talk. And she said: 'Pompey, I notice a great change in you; you are very sad. I feel it is about Freddy. But that will pass; but I know it is not easy, but to say: That will pass is not at the moment comforting at all, but it is true. When I think of you now Pompey I see something that is sad and stormy and I am very anxious for you. Your whole life Pompey is very sad.'

How sweet and serious Josephine is. There is something very sweet about her so that I am not furious when she says: Your life is very sad, I am not at once ferocious and affronted.

How sweet Josephine is, and now in a moment she has said this and I feel that indeed my life is very sad, but it is not a feeling of bitter sadness I have, it is as if together we were looking at something from the outside. It is not my life at all from the inside, but a Life of Pompey that we are for the moment looking at together. And it is for us both from the outside sad, in the way that the lives of

Maurice Baring's ladies are often so sad, for the sake of making the pattern that will please and satisfy the desire of their creator – and to hell with the reader.

But also it is rather funny in this way. Because this strong and forceful Josephine has created her picture of Pompey, and has for the moment projected it upon my vision, so that I forget the gay light moments, and the raffish black and hateful demon that runs alongside, and think only of this pure element of sadness that is quiet and touching and in its quality eternal.

But in the real sadness of désespoir there is a rushing tearing quality of unquietness that drives to death; it is this unquietness from which we may pray for deliverance and, not finding it, turn again to death that is so quiet. So that when the Josephine of the moment has gone, again the experience and knowledge of this actual sadness of life is borne in upon us, the sadness that brings one to speak to oneself and cry again: soll ich niemals wieder ruhig sein? Everybody must be quiet, and if they cannot come to it they are better dead.

I look round at my darling friends. Each one has patched up for herself a peace and an integrity where they can be quiet. They have put up this tent in their wilderness. They are not altogether happy but only so much so as they have made for themselves this tent of quietness. And some have done this better than others. And for me it is still something that I must find, must come at or die.

But what use contempt and scorn and self-hatred that has for its unstable foundation a feeling of guilt in the mishandling of a personal relationship. Friendship may be so mishandled, if one is weak and one is strong, the strong will overbear the weak. In love, ah in love, where everything is raised at once to extremity, and hate taps close aheel? Then there is no end to the injury and the cruelty of force and coercion upon unsuitability, and no end to the hatred and contempt and the feeling of guilt that will be for these darker emotions at once a cover and an excuse.

Hatred and contempt, what harm they have done to me and how gladly I would be quit of them. And to him, to Freddy? Pushed and driven against his wont, beyond his capacity, outside of his integrity? No, I am not so conceited to say that to Freddy, the harm is as great as to me.

I will tell you now, as quickly and shortly as possible I will tell you, that you will know why this book is set to anger and disturbance, and need not pity me.

Oh Pompey, I am so sick of bloody Freddy. Pax, Reader, see me through this and then no more of it.

I have forced a reconciliation upon Freddy. But wait, there is something a little bit funny about this something that has happened. My darling Freddy and I are reconciled. Then why is there still such a spate of stormish sadness and dirge? Oh why, for why ever? My darling Freddy and I are reconciled. And I must laugh and laugh, indeed it is funny.

Oh quiet now, quiet. Oh how I detest you Pompey, oh how detestable you are, I am sick to death of you, you abominable Pompey that has twisted everything the wrong way from the very beginning, that must torment this poor Freddy, this darling and affectionate and once so happy Freddy, your love, your darling, your sweetie-pie; that only must love you, and for this be torn to pieces, this little Freddy boy that only loved you, that only asked to love you and be loved. Oh how abominable you are Pompey, how I hate you. Oh to the stake and faggots with you, you abominable witch, I cannot now for one moment endure to think about you ever again.

But now I tell you there is something a little bit funny about all this that has happened to this black and devouring Pompey, this detestable witch, that is perhaps not so much a witch, with her little petty-pie familiar, her Freddy-Manilian, but that is going further back and getting blacker and darker je weiter es geht.

For I think of my name that is this Casmilus, that is the name of a great devil that laid waste the hearts of the people of Carthage before ever the Romans came with their conquering legions and their sacred ploughs to plough up the ruins of that accursed city that never more might its black walls rise to affront the imperial eagle. And I think of this devilish Casmilus, that never by an oversight got into the mind of Milton when he went to setting up aloft in hell so many of the great devils of antiquity, that time he was writing his satanic verse to set up on high the great devils that were overthrown to be set up again only by him and by Crashaw too when he must write about Lucifer that he was

> The judge of torments and the king of tears
> He fills a burning throne of quenchless fire

making to seem, do you see, that there was something sweet about this boy, that had his trials and crosses like the rest of us, but noble in defeat and somehow splendid, chaps, just splendid. And you get to think the way that God is punk, with no heart at all, and no fine sentiment for these noble failures that had these burning thrones of quenchless fire, and no other asset at all that you could think of, to put beside the high security of heaven's walls, towers, harps, seas, jasper and chalcedony.

But reading these poets, and sensing the magnificent power of this swift-running, counter-running, wrong ever wrong magic of their poetic vision, the sympathy of the reader too, if he has in him anything that is to make a response to the power of their verse, has to go running in this contrary current, that goes sweeping and licking up in a way that is contrary to truth and an abomination; but a sweet abomination and a very exceedingly delicious contrariness that is at the same time so dangerous.

For suddenly running swiftly after this deceitful sweetness of the verse, you go to running too far, too far, too far altogether, and suddenly you come to where it is getting dark, and very excessively dark and gloomy are these parts. And perhaps then suddenly you are there, and you are there. And there too are suddenly these great devils. And no, absolutely, there is nothing noble-in-defeat about them at all, nothing sweet, nothing to be desired.

Oh no, Pompey, now careful. Don't let mighty Milton and this sweet Crashaw, and the others that are setting up to go after them, conducting these parties to the grim underworld, don't let them go to conducting your soul on this famous intourist party. Remember the so-famous first conductor of conducted parties, the great Trismegistus, whose name by a punic sleight is yours, who was himself the only one of these conducted parties that ever, laughing softly up his sleeve, came back again from hell. So remember and remember to be wary and watchful.

Now I will tell you more of this reconciliation with

dear Freddy, and all of the something funny that it has brought with it. And at the end I will tell you the secret of it which is perhaps nothing to do with witchcraft or darker devilry but with something that has to do with my own convenience and is none the more presentable for all that.

To begin with there was for us again all of the lovely countryside of Hertfordshire for our walks together. Now I suspect that for me Hertfordshire is the operative word, and you have yourself no doubt already suspected this for a long time. Oh lovely Hertfordshire, so quiet and unassuming, so much of the real countryside, so little of beastly overrated bungaloid Surrey-Sussex with all of its uproar of weekend traffic to and from Bloomsbury, Hertfordshire is my love and always has been, it is so unexciting, so quiet, its woods so thick and abominably drained, so pashy underneath, if you do not know the lie of the land you had better keep out. Yes, I think anyway, you had better keep out. You can run for miles in Monk's Green Woods and never see a soul, and you can lie in the bracken and watch the bailiff go by and wish his gun to go off on him. But darling little Freddy since the reconciliation is growing bolder, and is so bold to say he is getting sick of Hertfordshire and wants a change. Hurra three times, bully for you, my boy! But I am become very meek and explorative of this sturdy attitude of cher

Freddy. So where shall we have our nice change? Hertfordshire can sit back and laugh; Hertfordshire can bide its time; so we go to Hadley Wood. Hadley Wood, gentle Reader, is a built-up area with a wood in the middle. It is a change.

But I am so meek and docile now; So what shall we do now dear Freddy for our change? So what have you got up your sleeve this time honey? Bottle Green. So we walk around this chic residential suburb and I do not suggest anything, I do not speak, I am so interested now to follow, follow, follow, and to tuck it away in my memory, indeed I cannot forget, and to remember. We walk round the blocks, chaps, round and around; and we walk into a park, but oh, it is not into the most beautiful of all parks that is this beautiful Scapelands Park, with its wide wild lake, its adorable dark lake, its woods and grasslands its unspoiled wild beauty, its moorhens, reedy pools, swans and the summer's second crop of cygnets. Oh no, we very carefully avoid Scapelands Park, and I am rather glad, do you know, I am glad that Scapelands is to be set aside this passage to sit back with county Hertfordshire, and laugh, and wait, and laugh.

We needs must love the highest when we see it. Chaps, there is no such compulsion. It is a figment of the mind poetical. Thank you Freddy for teaching me that.

But really Freddy I am not so cross. I am only very interested to explore this bold Freddy that can express his preferences. And I will follow you round – for a while.

Do you see the funny thing that is happening? I am no longer forcing the situation. And as my control, my wretched bully-driving that I am so ashamed of, slackens, he takes his gentle way, and I follow, follow after, observing, disliking, assessing. Phew, this is pretty steep. Yes, I know.

It is like, it is perhaps just *rather* like this. Well, imagine that it is a sunk submarine from which you will escape. But first you must stand quietly and without panic until the flood-water in the escape-room is covering your shoulders, is creeping up to your mouth, and only then when the whole of your escape-room is flooded to drowning point will you be able to shoot up through the escape-funnel, to shoot up for ever and away. You will have made a good escape. So this is Science, make no mistake. And in my mishandled love-situation, in this bitter commotion of feeling, for me it is much the same. Not until I am flooded with a dislike pointing to hatred can I escape, can I shoot up for ever and away. Yes it is like this. Well, rather like this. But I must escape from him, must get completely free of him. Oh, but this is the best way. Best for him and best for me.

In the gloaming,
Oh my darling,
Think not bitterly of me.

My noble aunt used as a girl I believe to sing this grand old song. Very affecting it must have been. I like to think of my noble Lion-Aunt, in a sentimental mood of an evening thus commemorating the suitors, already no doubt devoured in wrath and digested at leisure.

In the gloaming,
Oh my darling,
Best for you and best for me.

You see, darling Freddy, what your little lambie-pie is up to? She is up to no good, to not one good thing at all.

But there have been earlier moments of close rapprochement and release from the tide of hate that is set to flood.

In the London and North-Eastern Railway carriages, those delightful museum pieces that take you right back into the middle of the factory laws and the chimney-sweeping babies of the 'thirties and 'forties, to link up maybe with colds in the head, antimacassars, muffins for tea and evensong, in these antique compartments Freddy and I have often had a very close and comforting rapprochement.

It is the sickly green gaslight that does it. I am

partial, in my Mrs. Humphrey Wardish way, to sickly green gaslight. I like to have the smuts thick on the windows, the glass broken in front of some Gothic hotel, photographed in sepia and overscrawled with obscenity. I like to have the horsehair stuffing coming out of the cushions and over all and everything I will have a patina of railway dust. In such a setting, half suffocated by the fumes of sulphur from the tunnel in which we always stop, I have no rightmindedness about social intercourse, I am wholly Freddy's.

The purlieus of Kings Cross and the Pentonville Road, and that ominous dark lane that runs to the side of the suburban platform, have seen us too, late at night-times, under the gas lamps to meet. And then, under the green gaslight he is looking suddenly so lost and betrayed, so somehow sweet, I think, I must hug him a little he is looking so sweet.

So that, alas, we do not know whether we are coming or going, whether we should laugh or cry. He is lost, wounded and betrayed by that last old-fashioned hug and kiss under the eddying and unnatural flickering light of these poison green gaslights of the Pentonville Road. So that is what this detestable Pompey has done to her poor Freddy. He does not know whether he is coming or going.

When I am working, there is a man, he is a sort of Foreign Office runner, a messenger, a man that has a hard life to try and find the right magnate to sign the cheques, that is what they have to sign, that is such a really solid piece of their life-work to sign. And what else do they do but to say: 'Good-morning, Miss Casmilus, – *any news?*' Lord Victor Moan says this to me, raising his hat to say with a long eager hungry look, '*Any news?*'

Nothing but the wind blowing and the green grass growing. That is all that there is of all that there is to-day.

'Good-bye Miss Casmilus, I am just off to Hampshire for the weekend.'

'Good-bye Lord Victor. Did you see that an errand-boy fell in the ocean off Trevose Head and got drowned?'

I save up these pieces of news to tell Lord Victor, that has no wife to love and nourish him, to make him a more happy man; there is something sad and hungry about this lord, he looks like people never told him anything.

So one day there was the so grand piece of news about the washplace. This is the washplace that was first to be used only by Sir Phoebus and his brother, very grand and exclusive was this washplace snobismus. But presently Lord Victor was to use it too, and by and by, vilely and insidiously and with a *resolved conscience*, there were others coming creeping up the stairs to use this grand retreat.

So at this moment Sir Phoebus was in Budapest. So, No, I said, we were to have keys cut and to keep a look out and to be very ingenious and alert.

So Lord Victor that from being a gatecrasher had now become a foundation member of the washplace cabal, he was very happy and enthusiastic about this secret key thought of mine, and: 'Quite right,' he said, 'Quite right, Miss Casmilus, we can't have every Tom Dick and Harry using it.'

That you may see for yourself is how classism and cliqueism and snobism are set up to grow a strong and flourishing plant, and how sweet are the uses of privilege to the man that has something sad about him that comes from having people tell him nothing, and no wife to love and nourish him.

The other also has this way to say: *Any news?* But he is thinking of a different sort of news that comes hissing and bubbling over the telephone, that comes may be from the east side of us, from the great centres of the Stock Exchange and from the grand and sombre and fantastic riches of the City of London. Or that comes it may be perhaps from the west side of us, from the suave and evasive elegants in Whitehall, who have sometimes the great pleasure to tell us that, Yes, No, they are very sorry, but that particular tract of British territory is no longer governed from here but has its own legislative body, to whom the question must be referred direct. This is a retort of great chagrin to the Empire Builder. Oh we do not so much like to hear this piece of news at our end of the telephone.

But yesterday Sir Phoebus was looking very fetching indeed in dark dark mourning clothes and a dark dark top hat. So when the funeral was over he came back and said: 'Another good man buried.'

And this time it was old Lord Pevensey that was sixty-seven. So all the afternoon there was Sir Phoebus singing softly and happily in his own room, with the wide coal fire burning brightly in the grate with the brightness they have on these frosty days that have come to an end to-day, to give place to this oppressive winter heat and mist and smoke that come beating down upon all the narrow ways of Fleet Street and its alleys.

And what is he singing softly softly in his own room? Well then, he is singing 'For all the Saints', very soft and winning.

But Sir Phoebus is a young man and cannot come to have all of the joy that Lord Victor must have to hear that this great Lord Pevensey that is only sixty-seven is dead, and that he that is ten years older, is alive alive-oh.

The messenger that comes to the office to get his cheques signed, it may be by Lord Victor, it may be by Sir Phoebus, he is driven nearly distracted to find so often that the lord and the baronet are neither of them to be found. God bless my soul, he is nearly in tears, because the other baronet that lives round the corner, and also has this grand power to sign cheques, he is also nowhere to be found, and no one can say for certain where to lay the finger on him.

Oh it is very dreadful for this poor messenger, that has his living to earn, and a wife and children to support upon it. 'Oh Miss Casmilus,' he says, '*I do not know whether I am coming or going.*'

Now this phrase takes my fancy, oh how it does appeal to me, oh what a painful situation to be in, oh how essential for all comfort of body and soul to know beyond a shadow of a doubt that one is coming or that one is going. Oh it is the very first distinction about which the human mind distressed has a right to demand an absolute certainty. But you see this poor distracted messenger is deprived of this certainty, and with it there is made upon the essential dignity and privilege of his humanity a most perilous attack. *I do not know whether I am coming or going.*

And this you see is what the abominable Pompey has done to the precious relationship between her sweetie-pie and herself. So that drifting like Paolo and Francesca (who may well themselves have made use of this pregnant phrase) along the gaslit haunts of the waifs of Euston Road and St. Pancras, we have come to it to say, Indeed we do not know whether we are coming or going, whether we should laugh or cry, that now again we have before us all of that Hertfordshire excursion to do again, the pubs and teashops to visit, the church-yards to explore, the hedgerows to sit beside, with all of the deep dark impenetrable forest for our playground.

But the rhythm of good-bye is in my blood and I am set again for foreign parts. I know very well dear Freddy that I am *going*, and I know where I am going. And the lips that were so treacherous to kiss you, it was to say good-bye.

My darling friend Harriet is giving a party.

I am lying now on the divan in her flat, lying back on the cushions, glancing through the shadows and the flickering firelight at the faces of the friends and the friends of the friends of Harriet. It is very restful, really for once we are not talking so much. Reggie holds my hand in a quiet trance. He is lying beside me on the divan. It is very quiet.

I am now feeling so sad and quiet with the thoughts that go helter-pelter through my mind. They are making me so tired. I am so wishing for a moment that they were not there, do you know, that the mind of Pompey was as empty and as spick and span as a new washed saucepan.

Do you ever have the thought, gentle Reader, the thought to have an empty mind, to be like the clam that sits upon the mud in the sunlight, without the burden of this voracious consciousness that goes to eating up everything it sees and hears to make up a thought about it?

You must be receptive to your own thoughts, said I to the great established and polished man of letters that sat having lunch with me one fine day, after a couple of bottles of Liebfraumilch. This man was certainly a silent man in the beginning, not one word, not one single word to ease a situation that was becoming rather acutely painful, these long silences that beget longer silences, till it is like you would burst.

But presently, getting into the second bottle of Liebfraumilch, and, Here's to us, old chap, we began to find we were both of us having a lot of brilliant and unusual things to say, and these brilliant remarks (it was a pity there was no one there to make a book out of them) got to coming out at the same moment. So with no offence, no offence in the world, there we were both of us talking together, and going at it like we would never stop.

So here it was I came out with this clever idea that if you are going to write, and then why certainly you must go on writing, and above all you must be receptive to your own thoughts.

But now I feel that you must be very careful about this clever idea, or you will go to opening a door that never never will it be shut again. And all these ideas that have by this time got so upstage and unruly, they will come rushing in at you from the outside-of. And heaven must help you in that last situation, for all else is all up with you then, and you will have put yourself under a tyranny that will make Hitler look like the lady-companion that advertises in the *Church Times* for her keep, her bed-oh, with five shillings a week pocket-money, Catholic Privileges and Indoor Sanitation.

Well now, is it not sad? Why now certainly this Pompey is becoming very sad-case and dippy, for see now I am crying, yes the tears are coming out plop and rolling down my cheeks, to think of these thoughts that have so many behind them, coming rolling in with the long rolling surges of the Pacific Ocean up against the Australian coastline; with so many thoughts, crested and predatory, coming rolling up alongside, and behind them out to sea a whole ocean of thoughts to come rolling and slithering up the beach of consciousness. Oh there will perhaps not be time for all the thoughts, all that great wilderness of thought, coming rolling up from the deep deep sea.

So with Reggie lying beside me on the divan, suddenly I sit up and turn away from him, and look round the room of Harriet's flat, to think about the room and keep my thoughts from the thoughts.

First of all I must think about the Lion Vase that is no longer upon the mantelshelf. When Harriet gives one of her lovely parties, she takes down the Lion Vase that stands on her mantel overshelf, this Lion Vase that she brought with her from her house in Athens, smuggling it out of Greece with great adroitness, this registered ancient Lion Vase that is more than two thousand years old, she takes it down, and puts it safely away behind the fabric curtains of the alcove. And there the Lion Vase sits in shrouded safety. But to-night Harriet's party is not so wild that Lion Vase might fear for his great age, that has brought him down from ancient times to be a registered memorial and a prohibited export.

This animal, this lion, (I will describe for you), he is walking round the base of the vase. He has puffed out the pads of his paws. With great precision he places them upon the ground. He turns his head making a delicate *moue*; he is in a quiet mood you would say, he is walking there quietly, a little abstracted, in the jungle evening perhaps. He is a serious animal in middle life. Only his tail is a little wild. This tail is very vivid, very tense with an upward rake and twist that has a suggestion of something that is wicked. Looking at that lion I should say now at once, Beware of the quiet lion with the rogue tail walking quietly in the jungle evening. Be careful not to cross the path of this serious middle-aged lion, that is turning his head, that has this funny look upon his lion face.

Beautiful Lion Vase, sombre and ferocious lion, so set in upon himself, so quiet and aloof. And quiet horse of my earlier picture-gallery excursion, set in again in quietness upon a sombre ferocity. Ah, the animals *are* so quiet. There is no fuss up there, no fret and fume for guilt and delinquency, no mind sickness and a thought upon death.

Reggie puts his arm around me, I think he is getting rather bored. Stephen lies upon the floor. He is such a sweetie-pie for Harriet, this Stephen, and there is something sad about him and sweet. Though I think, Is this sadness perhaps a cloak of interesting romanticism that he is wearing? Mourning becomes Electra, this dark cloak of sadness becomes Stephen. He certainly looks swell in this cloak, very distinguished, arrogant, and glum, chaps, glum. Stephen lies on the floor, getting rather hot and sick feeling, with being so near to the elegant gas stove as all that, he gets sick. But then he is in a stupor, he cannot move, but must get hotter and sicker. That is a curious state to be in, that he cannot move away from the fire that is making him sick.

It is near Christmas time now and this is a Christmas party. Presently we have some more drinks. And now we are going on to dance at the house of a friend in St. John's Wood. So we are going on.

I am feeling real unearthly ill.

So now we are going on.

There is a Christmas feeling in the air that is so damp and mild. There is a feeling of the shining bright dark witch-balls that dandle from the crisp tinsel ropes. Green and red and steel blue they hang there in the damp close mild December afternoon.

The windows are wide open against the damp late sky. In the garden are the cedar trees, and the dark evergreen close-growing bushes. We run out on to the pavements. It is so curiously hot and steamy, so enervating to the body, so over-stimulating to the mind, and to the nerves and the thoughts, that keep such uneasy dance within the mind, the thoughts that go helter-pelter, shattering and scattering the peace of God that passeth all understanding, that never shall I come to know again, this outcast and abominable Pompey that is now sitting on Reggie's knee in the close dark taxi, pressing against this stranger Reggie, that is kind, and has his own troubles, and is a stranger.

So now we come to the house of the friend in St. John's Wood. This is a very large house. It is a house of enormous rooms. Already there are many people there, they are dancing. The rooms are lighted by electric candles in wall sconces, the lights are very soft. Very languorous and lingering is the light as it falls upon the faces of the women. The faces seem so pale, so frail, so unsubstantial, raised in rapt attention to the bowed and shadowed faces of the partners. There is something a little disturbing in this rapt attention, this silence in the soft soft light.

Oh where now is Harriet – my rock, my foundation, my refuge, my secure Harriet, my security to stand between me and the thunder stone, the great thunder stone to come dropping down, dropping in silence and immensity from the sultry Christmas skies, from the smoky upper air, where all is storm and confusion, disaster and malice and a false imagining?

'Harriet, Harriet!'

'Why, what is the matter, Pompey?'

The smiling gracious face of Harriet is smiling down upon me.

'Why it is nothing. Why what is it, what can it be? Here is Reggie and Stephen, and here am I.'

Here am I.

But the face, the dear faces, vanish. It was a

moment for a dream to think, We are all here, it is all right.

There is something of an acute pain of cruelty in this, to think for the moment it is certainly all very slap-up and o.k. There is no one there at all. I run through the immense, the enormous room, there is no one there at all. But there is the idea of laughter running after and before me. So there is music too. So coming suddenly into a wide and lofty room, whose ceiling I cannot seem to see, it is so far away, so shadowed and remote, I must begin to dance.

Oh now this is lovely, this is very swift and exhilarating. So I dance, faster and faster. And now faster again, with long wrenching outward movements, the long wrenching outward movements you have when you are under the anaesthetic, under the anaesthetic. And you dance and dance, with an intensity of concentration, an exaltation, an exhilaration of the spirit, and at centre a heart of darkness, of darkness and désespoir.

But the music grows faster, more slave-driving, more compelling. There is no rest, no pause. There are so many evolutions to be performed, evolutions, revolutions, and so little time. Quickly, quickly, correctly and meticulously, I turn, I chassée, I curtsey, dipping, turning, straining straining upwards and backwards. And always there is this pain at my heart that I cannot bear, cannot bear. Oh really it is more than is possible, it is not to be borne, this pain at my heart that is so rending and tearing, and always getting more and more. And within the music there is moving now a more insistent clamour, a harsh grating sound, a clashing of steel on steel. It is very menacing, very military, this rapidly increasing metallic clamour, thrusting, driving, marching.

Oh player of this sad, tearing and distracting music, can you not understand that it cannot be borne for one moment longer.

Oh chords of immensity and insistence, waves of conflict from some deep hidden ocean bed, deep beyond depths so hidden and so secret, sweeping up, licking and stretching, to cover and engulf some lonely seagirt promontory, come cover over then and make an end.

I am borne upright, suspended in the fathomless deep waters of a sombre and phosphorescent sea, swinging in silence and desolation between the poles of the world. How silent and sombre the deep swinging sea, swinging in malevolent intent upon its own storm basis of volcanic fury, what depths above me and below, how hellishly cold it is, how bitter and how solitary.

There is certainly this to be said for pain, the sort that you can spell with a capital p, it is a white hot bright scorching flame that takes a girl right out of herself, that is up to that moment getting morbid thinking her own troubles are the only troubles in a world, that is just trouble from the first screech of the baby bursting from the belly to cry out aloud in the voice and incidence of the thin steel blade he must be if he is to be anything at all in this life of trouble but the little funny that goes backwards and forwards smelling of *Untergrundbahnhof* and season tickets. Bursting then as I said from the womb, he cries aloud to let all know he is not to be this strap-hanging season-ticket holder, not just this, but perhaps this too, but with something else added to him that is to give him pride and integrity, so he cries: I have thrown away the scabbard. And may he never hark back again ever at all to that safe womblandish scabbard but go right forward and be a shining bright sword and maybe a disaster, if it comes to it he may be this disaster, but he will not be a little bloody squit that only asks please not to be noticed but to let pass in the crowd.

When I got down after getting shot up with this pain in my heart that was getting me shot up on to that blazing phosphorescent night sea that was going swinging swinging in mighty aloofness and pride between the poles of the world, I got sitting down on the floor of this room in this high class house in St. John's Wood, and sitting down there I was certainly now feeling like a piece of whipcord, thin trailing seaweed that has been mulcted of its iodine content and left alone by tide and man alike to abandonment on the upper beach that never a blasted – You – know – could put in his smart column to make a few words and a hell of a lot of dollars. I got thinking about pain.

There are some writers, I name no names, that make a lot of money writing about pain, pain is to them an inexhaustible fount of inspiration and a regular income. Specially nowadays, when people are getting so strung up and enervated full of fatigues and unrest by reason of the motor bicycles the electric drills and the radio, is this subject of the splendidness of primitive great chaotic pain a favourite to come in first and leave the field at the starting gate.

There was once when I was sitting in a Great Northern Railway carriage plying between Kings Cross and Hertford North there was this little man that was sitting next me in the corner of the second class carriage that was reading a book. It was like he was ashamed of reading this book. Very refined and shy he was about showing this book that he was reading, keeping it turned covers upwards, do you see, so that it was real difficult for me to get a look at its title. Whereas most people that travel in second class railway carriages, what with *The Times*, the *Daily Telegraph*, the *News Chronicle*, *Without My Cloak* and *Oliver Entwhistle*, it is so you can take your choice and who cares?

It is certainly to be said that on these railway journeys if you don't want to read, and are real set on not reading come what may, you are going to have a great difficulty to sit thinking and thinking and not to have the printed word thrust under your nose. So many printed words, phew it is hard if you are like me and like to sit wrapped up in thoughts about your dear friends and how they are and how they are, sinking your own troubles in the friends of the friends, sink me if it is not.

It is better to be like Father Time in that great poem that Hardy wrote, that little boy who sat in the railway carriage with his ticket in his hat. There he sat with his feet dangling thinking forlorn thoughts, this poor little boy, that would have moved the bowels of compassion of a lesser poet than T. H. This was the little boy that later hung up his relations-by-marriage in a cupboard leaving a note on the pincushion to say Done Because We Were Too Many. See?

Now those damned bloodsuckers the commentators will say this is a pretty punk author that gets the poem *The Boy in the Third Class Railway Carriage* mixed up this way with *Jude the Obscure*. But to hell with it, it takes an artist to appreciate an artist and the basest of all the hangers-on of artistic creation are these same commentators that are always so smart to point out what's what and how the comma got left out and the quotation misquoted. To hell with them.

Last night I went to dinner with a young dryasdust that has a charming wife. Well may be anyway the young dryasdust as the years go by will shed some of his academic suet pudding that sits so heavy on the stomach. But to the moment he can do nothing but be this dryasdust that covers the living limbs of the poets with the vile slime of commentary, so dull, so pompous, so without hope and so cruel in its stupidity. Why he must even go to translating the Germans that had better be let drop in the brook with the stone around their necks than to go sullying the clear stream of inspiration and increasing the bright pains of creation with such dreary nonsense. Oh it makes me sick. They are the bagmen of the arts that should give themselves airs with their slants and slopes and tendencies and time-sequential tyrannies. And when they will be so bright and breezy with such ready ready wisecracks and funny bits, like they do now, the older ones do, that have got to carrying their beastly fustian with all the airs and graces of the Queen of Love and Beauty, oh they should be sent to the back, of the column with all the rest of the cooks and scullions and bag-carriers and given a kick in the pants to keep them in their place. Oh to hell with them.

There was this little boy that was sitting dangling his feet in the railway carriage thinking his own forlorn thoughts, and keeping them to himself in a quiet and dignified way an adult might do worse than imitate. And did he bother to go thinking what his neighbours were reading, maybe sitting so jammed tight that he was overlapped and submerged in the printed pages his fellow travellers were so ready to thrust upon him? He did not. And maybe anyway had he wanted to he couldn't, because maybe he couldn't read, but I like to think it was from delicate and deliberate choice he occupied himself quietly with his own thoughts sitting there wrapped in dignity he might have been an Emperor.

But here in my case now I guess I was at fault, for the more the man beside me in the corner, the more and the more he tried to conceal what it was that was so holding his attention to read and not to be overlooked, so the more did I make no bones at all to overlook and to wait and to bide my time. So presently, so entrancing was this book he was reading that by and by in an incautious moment down fell the flaps of the book, and there it was plain and high class in beautiful typography, *The Pleasures of the Torture Chamber*. And to offset it on the further page was an ingenious illustration of a human being suffering an extremity of torment and indignity.

Oh what pleasure can there be in this that stinks of the slums of hell and is the very spit of the fiend?

There are many reasons why it is and why it is. Sometimes it is because people are so dumb cluck on the sentient plane, they have a very high flash point, they need a burning fiery furnace heated seventy times seven before their cold damp insentiency can catch alight-o. These are the subhumans, the people that go to throng the Coliseum when the lions are on show with the Christians, and who go to throng the cinemas when there is some tough work in the prisons of the U.S.A., or maybe it has a political excuse, and it is photographs of atrocities by Abyssinians, or maybe it is negro-baiting across the Atlantic, or maybe it is *The Fall of St. Petersburg* and again with the prison brutality that is so the most beastly of all, so shut in and without all hope.

Oh this is a very desperate and bitter cruelty that exacerbates and affronts our immortality, that brings all to nothing to negation and betrayal. Avoid it.

Oh in this desperate cruelty and pain wherein the mind is darkened and the flesh set in domination above the spirit, oh in this there is all the abomination of reversal and traduction in the backward going and the darkening and the death of the spirit. It is contrary to nature and abominable.

And to exploit it and to contrive so to make a sensation, that is the abomination of the intellect that is dried out and rotten, with only the dry bones of the intellect, and no flesh and no blood of the spirit, no fire and exaltation but only a knowingness and a great tiredness.

So. Look at Whatshisname. We will call him Sam. Sam certainly is the clever boy. Why look at all that's set down here about chemical reactions and about the science of medicine. There is the child that died of cerebral meningitis. It is all so carefully, so painstakingly described, to make you sick, to make you sick, since the writing is so dead awful, so like the magazine story that is a good second class woman's magazine story. Well, you *got* to have some emotion, and what easier than to make people go having that sick feeling in the pit of the stomach by a long trail of medical detail that is so nauseating to those that are not of the profession, so easy, so easy. Say you're feeling dead, just dead and frozen in the emotions, just so much dead matter functioning mechanically, catching trains and eating your food-oh just like you were an automaton? Well, there you are, take a look at this word painting that goes to show the viscera stripped of all concealing curtains, and feel the black bile rising in you.

Hurra, hurra. This is life. Now I am alive again that can feel simply sick. Now I am alive again that was dead.

And there is the cruelty of it too, the cruel descriptions to bring the cruelty more before you, to shake you up and give you a reaction, like it was the doctor striking below the knee-cap of the crossed leg. That's science, chaps, make no mistake.

This cruelty is very much in the air now, it is very dangerous, it is a powerful drug that deadens as it stimulates. And if the leaders of intellect will have truck with it, what hope for the crowd? Oh, just the hope that is in the crowd always, to save them by their stupidity from the gross injury the leaders will operate upon themselves to hand down to their children.

But when you read what Sam says you have all the time the feeling that Sam knows a lot, and Sam is clever, but that Sam is tired and should quit writing.

There are dreams that come to us in the night that are full of cruelty. And the effect of cruelty upon the imagination is fear. And the result of fear is death. There is nothing noble in this, it is something hateful and to be endured and to be resisted.

I sometimes feel there is nothing noble in this book at all, but just sadness and tears and death without glory. And perhaps it is I should quit writing, and not that Sam I was speaking of just now, that has this world weariness about him but can set out so many many pages of words that go to tell the story.

Now in this last book of Sam's I read it is interesting now how it is. There are so many stories in this one book that are looking a bit like melodramas. There is to begin with the melodrama of the boys' school that is like *The Fifth Form at St. Dominic's*. Only with nothing left to the imagination. And so by this trick you see, by putting in all the words that So-and-So left out, and all the descriptions of What every boy knows, it goes to lifting the schoolboy melodrama right out of So-and-So's class. My dear this is 1936. But all the same it is all the same.

And there is the melodrama of the good white man bearing the white man's burden (that is a medicine chest this time) round and about the primaeval forests of darkest South America, kiss me Dr. Hardy and I die fulfilled.

And there is the melodrama of the Sorrows of Werther and the troubles of Mrs. Haliburton – only it is Mr. Haliburton this time and the self-lacerations of the hero. And there is the melodrama of the desert of unhappy love, and the melodrama of any fair light lady that might be Becky Sharp, brought to book and bed in old age, with the morphia or the whisky or whatever it is, sitting up in bed. With all of the description of dirt and disease and the survival of the sex urge beyond the climacteric to give you once again that lovely exhilarating pussy-not-feel-well upheaval in the pit of the stomach.

So many writers do you see, so many writers' thoughts, so much of English literature, melodramatized. And over and above and underneath it all the great red herring of the broken time sequence to cover up and conceal the bare bones that will not live again, pipe he never so sourly.

Oh cover up conceal and forget. Ah sweet oblivion of the *Quit writer quit*.

But oh again the too easy stimulus of applied torture, the Pleasures of the Torture Chamber. Evvivant viscera!

And who is this Pompey that is sitting melancholy in a corner? Who is this miserable Pompey, hugging her own distraction, that she should say: Quit. With her own pain heavy on her hand and the memory of dreams to wake crying: Oh no. Oh no. No, no, no. That is the rhythm of the dream, to cry aloud, to wake in the empty house the echoes of the thrice repeated dissent, to awaken the lionlike aunt who sleeps in peace strength and integrity, to rouse the Lion of Hull to come pouncing down upon the word.

When I awake,
The whole returning flood of consciousness is hateful to me,
And death too often on my lips, Becomes my shadower,
Oh death, death, death, Deceitful friend,
Come pounce, And take,
And make, An end at once.

From what impalpable dream of refusal with no power of refusal am I awakened to palpable dismay and death-driven repudiation? I do not wish to consider, to explore, to recall again the dream that now lives only in effect.

But see, about this boy Sam, this clever boy, there is something of the *voyeur* – Oh he must see and examine and think upon the very *Materialismus* of cruelty. With minute attention to the most painstaking detail, he will have it all set out and presented.

And it is an emptiness and a desert. As well go see the pictures behind the curtains at Nuremberg that Topaz was saying. I suppose it is something extra to pay to look at these grand exhibitions. These are the pictures that are drawn without inspiration, without art, just so laborious and so painstaking. It is that element of patient labour that is making you so sick.

But the great artist can touch cruelty and not

make you shudder sick and ashamed? But this is very interesting. There is then this division between the laborious cruelty-fan and the artist also with his artist's soul creating and brooding upon the darkness of pain?

Why yes certainly there is this division. But where is the line of severance? Ah yes where is it? This is already getting dangerous.

There is Goya that has an idea embracing but transcending the *crudelitas* that is in his Proverbs and his Disasters of War – *They have no hope*.

In the Spanish School of painting there is always latent this idea of pain. But it is rather the effect and not the detail, the idea and not the incidence of pain, that is there lit up, and firelit up, by the sombre night of the midnight thought of the Peninsula.

Is it not curious that during the Spanish occupation of the Netherlands not any of the great cruelty of the oppressor is mirrored in the great Netherlandish painters of the period? But in distant proud Spain, land of the oppressor and the conqueror, the great painters were then, as Goya so many years later, unable to avoid this cruelty, but must tip their paint brushes with the colours of physical agony to portray the more subtle agony of the spirit.

I am sitting here on the floor, leaning against the wall of this enormous room, my legs stretched out before me, legs that have twisted and turned, chasséed and turned again, so swiftly so enchantingly for me in my danse macabre, so recently, so exhaustingly; my legs are now stretched out quietly before me to take their ease.

And sitting here in this enormous room of this enormous house, in the dark December of St. John's Wood, I rest quietly, but tensed too to the thoughts that come rushing in, slanting down and in upon me, like the great gale-beaten seas of the south coast, beating up from the Old Harry rocks upon Josephine's cliffs and undercliffs.

And there is in my thoughts too the salt cold spray and the icy touch of the Christmas sea in these thoughts that come to me on this so interesting idea of Spanish and Dutch painting.

Ah pain, ah wilderness of pain and war and death. And throughout and outside of it all in the awful aloofness of the artist, the mind that creates and is aloof and by itself, alone with the loneliness that is so cold as death, more cold than the salt sea water lapping and sucking beneath the icebound waves of northern Russia.

Northern Russia. I must pause now to think of Ian Crawford, husband of my most dear friend Anna, who has the nice but rather cold house in Essex, they are friends of mine and of Josephine's. Ian, kindest and most simple and honourable of men, was an officer at 17 in the Battle of the Somme; at 20 in Russia, Archangel. There was this Alice in Wonderland Gefühl. Where is the enemy? Where is the O.C. to whom I must report? Where are my men, the stores, the billets? Ian, kindest of men, of fathers, of husbands, in that fantastic long night of Russian madness and enchantment; lost, lost, lost.

British officer loses men, loses billets, loses stores, loses Officer Commanding. Is British officer himself loser or lost, in that painful and prolonged absurdity of General Ironside's campaign?

Ian tells me about it. 'Pompey, we would have murdered our own grandmothers.'

Pompey was sitting by Anna's fireside, nursing little daughter Helen, aged three, fat and placid infant, round of eye, of face, of form, fat as butter, comfortable as a large tabby cat.

Ian tells me. All the Russians who helped the British, who even spoke to them, were seen talking to them, were packed off to an island in the White Sea, where they froze to death, saving their captors the expense of board and lodging, and the slighter expense of a bullet, delinquent truckling to humanitarianism. Cruelty à la Russe. Russians murder their British officers, desert to enemy (found at last). Reds put them in front line of attack. All recaptured by British and Australian troops who kill them, not shoot them but rip their stomachs up with bayonets. Cruelty à l'Anglaise. *We would have murdered our own grandmothers.* But battle cruelty. British do not maim or mutilate. (Uneasy ghosts stirring through the pages of our history.)

Maiming, mutilating, torturing, in the land of occupation, in the name of a creed that is diverse, for the sake of a different thought. Cruelty à l'Espagnole.

But Netherlandish muse approved in Spain, white flag of art respected by all combatants. Clemency à l'Espagnole.

But this so little stressing of the spiritual significance of cruelty in Netherlandish art. Compare again Goya – and to hell with the time factor. That little canvas of his in London, it is called 'The Bewitched.'

There is the man, he is looking a little bit mad you know, there is the wild look in his eyes, the foam flecks on his lips, he is calling aloud, he is holding up a lantern that casts its rays only a little to the right, to the left. And there faintly seen as on the borderland of dreaming sleep, faintly to be apprehended, to be guessed with what appal; is it? yes it is, it cannot be, it is, there, towering gigantic, are the mules and asses of memory reared up on their hind legs, ferocious of tooth, of heel, kicking, rearing, tearing, to come one minute more they will fall upon the world to rend it and tear it altogether in pieces.

The Spanish Christ. Here the type is nervous, highly strung, with a capacity for suffering that is beyond the body. Compare the Dutch Christ, the conventional suffering of the body, the conventional concession to the history and religious significance of the subject, and then – away with it all for the sturdy Dutch individualism, the delight in the particular, the contempt (once the obligatory concession is made) for all generalization; the national, the individual, the Dutch manner for the Dutch artist.

There can be no good art that is international. Art to be vigorous and *gesund* must use the material at hand. *Numen inest.* Oh the folly and weakness of foreign travel in search of inspiration. We carry our own wilderness with us, our emptiness or our fullness, no matter.

How much a dunce that has been sent to roam,
Excels a dunce that has been kept at home.

The spirit reacts on the body that houses it. Inspiration feeds upon the matter at hand. Genius touches the Is and enfolds the Was and the Shall Be.

Enfolds. How I like this word. I will put my thoughts in a lamb-fold, a gemütliche lamb-fold where they can be quiet. It is time.

'Have you ever had a great pain?' Said my schoolboy cousin to me one day, wishing to brag schoolboy-boyscout way of the pains that he had had. 'Have you ever been beaten?'

'Why no, Hughie darling, girls aren't you know,' said I, laughing a little. 'And does it hurt so-o-o much?'

'Oh yes, like hell it does,' says sweet Hughie, screwing up his nose to express the utmost of the pains of hell. He is flushed with pride to have come through deep waters not unscathed.

Have I ever had a great pain? Why no. I always have gas. My thoughts turn with civilized habilitude to the dentist's chair. My dentist, very skilled and gentle, is the kindest of men, he would not hurt a fly, he would not hurt Pompey. He had better not. Once trussed and gagged for extraction. 'Ga ga ga,' I cried. Patiently he removed the stuffing. 'Remember,' I shouted, very desperate, 'remember to give me enough gas: please remember that I take a lot of gas because last time they did not give me enough and I distinctly felt the feeling of a tooth that is not coming out so easily but is twisted at the root. So please to remember.' Back went the stuffing and the operation was performed under complete anaesthesia, I have no complaints.

But talking to my little cousin, now I remember, with great pride I recall and state that five times, five times I have sprained my knee.

'And did it hurt?'

Like hell, my sweet, for half of a split second, and then settled itself into a formidable swelling with water beneath the knee cap and icecold water dripping above it from an ice bag suspended in a cradle. And so laid me by the leg for seven long weeks. For me thus not the transfixion of pain, so dear to Hughie and the clever boy-Sams of this world, but only the longueurs of discomfort.

But this dividing line of ours between the cruelty that is art and the cruelty that is *feelthy pictures*, (But, Mister, I show you the *most* feelthy pictures), that is still so much to seek?

The New Testament narrative of the crucifixion is on the one side the supreme example, and there are poems in our literature, from the earliest times to the present day, that are worthy of it. At random there are these poems:

the hill is all bald stone
And now and then the hangers gave a groan
Up in the dark, three shapes with arms outspread

God, lord, it is a slow way to make die

that is the right side of the line, and you can read

the rest for yourselves, I have left the blanks deliberately, you can read it for yourselves, it is beautiful as a whole.

Then there is also this:

Large throne of Love! royally spread
With purple of too rich a red:
  Thy crime is too much duty;
  Thy burthen too much beauty;
Glorious or grievous more? thus to make good
Thy costly excellence with thy King's own blood.

and this:

The third hour's deafen'd with the cry
Of 'Crucify Him, crucify'.
So goes the vote (nor ask them, why?)
'Live Barabbas! and let God die.'
But there is wit in wrath and they will try
A 'Hail' more cruel than their 'Crucify'.
For while in sport he wears a spiteful crown,
The serious showers along His decent Face run sadly
  down.

and this:

Drop, drop, slow tears,
And bathe those beauteous feet,
Which brought from heaven
The news and Prince of peace.

Cease not, wet eyes,
His mercies to entreat;
To cry for vengeance
Sin doth never cease.
In your deep floods
Drown all my faults and fears;
Nor let his eye
See sin, but through my tears.

Oh how enchanting that last one is oh how I do love it, is it not ravishing – *the news and Prince of peace*. But is it not curious of these four poems that I have chosen two are by the same author and the three that I have chosen to set out in full are of the same period? Ah blessed seventeenth century that is striking in my ears as I say these lines over to myself, oh blessed seventeenth century that is so much the time for me, my favourite of all times of writing.

And on the other side of this dividing line? (for you see I will not let you escape the issue, nor myself either, that is so set to cross-trailing that must cross-trail to eternity if I do not come to heel). Then then, on the other side of the dividing line of pain-in-art and pain-in-madness-badness is nothing but Evvivant viscera, and the Oh no, Oh no, no, no, no, of the undeliberate dream that is to be endured and yet resisted, the horror of refusal with no power of refusal, Oh no, Oh no. No, no, no.

Pettish Reggie comes prancing into the large empty room, this enormous room where I am sitting on the floor fanning myself with my solar topee. Your *solar topee*, no really Pompey, this is the last straw. Neither the last nor the penultimate straw, Reader, did I not say that this party of Harriet's that went on and was and is this party in St. John's Wood, is a fancy dress party and I am dressed in khaki shorts and shirt, solar topee and sandals and representing the bounds – limit to you – of Empire? If I did not say this it is because I forgot. O.K. – that is a fault.

'We have been looking for you *everywhere*,' screams Reggie. 'Harriet is furious, *simply* furious.'

My darling Harriet is furious? It is but absolutely impossible. Unlike dear Freddy she has not these moods of easy and unsignificant fury.

'But Reggie, I was only sitting thinking for a moment. I guess I want a drink.'

So Reggie takes me by the arm and now we are slap up again and O.K. bang in the middle of the party that is now at twelve o'clock, and going on, and going on.

At the bar all is rush push and confusion, so by and by cross Reggie brings me a bronx and another and already I am feeling I am feeling. So presently things are getting better all round and it doesn't matter if some people – I name no names – are a bit dim dum mum and glum on their own. Taken in the crowd humanity's all right, there's nothing wrong with humanity.

That, dear Reader, as you will have observed for yourself is just what there is of just what there is of the difference between perfect sobriety and imperfect sobriety, just the reversal of the pie-eyed early morning dictum: Give me my friends and hang the crowd.

There is a critic drinking by the bar. He is fair fat famous and fifty, he is my pet aversion. He has a perpetual down on the young middle aged, the war generation, Oxford undergraduates and Londoners. He is, even at this moment I can hear him, blowing off about the so-bright boys and girls who are growing up in the provinces. Who cares? He must feel inferior, but these young people of his they are young and they are provincial and no back answers. Do you see? Such a lovely lovely audience for this masculine schoolmistress from . . . No you don't catch me out there. Such lovely discipular *Schwärmerei*. So much of Oh isn't he the sweet boy? Mr. Low-Down on Life is even now again blowing off on this fascinating extra special pet theme that is his pet theme urbi et orbi usque ad. But to think that the sweet boy will blow off for nothing that something he might get God knows what a line for in the Sunday papers. He certainly must be drunk.

Away from the bar at the back of the room where the stairway opens up and down is seated my elegant Harriet. There is Stephen beside her and opposite her is Igor Torfeldt the actor that is the darling of our costume drama fans. He has a sensitive face and at the moment is putting on no world sad lost despairing airs and graces, he is just lapping up some hock cup and leaning across to look at Stephen. And no wonder, for this darling little Stephen is looking very extremely confidential and teaching. He holds his audience spellbound. I am wondering, I am laughing a little to wonder what he is saying that is so informative and confidential to hold Igor Torfeldt and dear Harriet in such a toil. This sad sad Stephen, our little sweetie-pie, our Mourning-Becomes-Electra, I guess what he is saying is: This modern world of Sturm und Drang is so bed-botton false, so full of désespoir and the scent of death, so predestined to perdition, to life-in-death and eternal malaise, and the reason is that *Babies are Weaned too Soon.* Reader, I am not making this up; it is what he said. I have heard him say it.

No wonder the boy is so sad, I am sorry for his sadness. But what can I do to help him? Peptonized milk will not bring him again to that infant peace so rudely and untimely shattered.

The milk of our mothers' kindness has ceased to flow; and fascism, communism, Italy, Germany, Abyssinia, Japan, the failure of the banking system, the debunking of Adam Smith, follow follow follow, as B follows A, and the sweet donkey the carrot. There is nothing to be done about it, nothing at all, but nothing. So drink up my chicks and put a pretty face on it.

Igor Torfeldt do you know he looks awfully well in profile. He is a blond Jew, it is rather fascinating, that so-racial bonework of the face, and the blond blond hair and blue-grey eyes, yes, there is something sweet about this boy. I have a tendre for these blond Jew faces, they look so patient, so souffrant, so sicklied o'er, bleached, albinoed and depigmented, by What of the Sorrows of Werther by the Dark Tarn of Auber, With-Psyche-his-soul-and-nobody-to-hold-his-paddypaw.

I was once sitting in the stalls, (third row, press tickets) at a matinée performance of *Caution Deletes* in which sweet honey-bug Igor played the crucified lead.

Why he was being so crucified, so transfixed and crucified by the turn of fate, I do not remember, I guess it was a sort of private crucifixion, but crucified he was all right, with such a sad patient face. But only for the moment I can remember just nothing to account for it.

Matinées, with such idols as Igor playing lead, are happy hunting grounds for all old ladies, and two sat beside me. Over the teacups during the interval the one old girl was telling the other what Igor meant to her declining years. 'He is, I think, a Jew, but my dear, the very best type of young Jew – *like Our Lord.*'

This thus numbering of the Saviour with Igor among the best type of young Jew, the aristocracy of Israel, the people who count, the almost one of us, came as a sweet reward to my inquisitive ear. As William said to me the other day: If it wasn't for the audience, the theatres would be empty.

I have now had three . . . no four, no really I cannot tell . . . So presently up comes Edward Oldacre and takes me off. He is a pleasant man of forty-five, he lives in Devonshire, he loves hunting, he paints a little, pleasantly enough; I know his wife; they have six children. So this is a little haven of peace. We sit on top of the stairs and mock the guests. I set my topee beside me and drink out of two straws a lovely glass of ginger beer with an ice cream foaming and dissolving at the bottom. Fascinating drink! We have a little peace and chat. It is very relieving to sit beside kind Edward Oldacre and drink ginger beer and ice cream. Unfortunately Baldur Löwen has seen us. At the moment he is down below dancing with a young, a very young red-headed girl in a banal pierrette costume. Oh God, I guess I wish I could get Edward away before the dance is over, but Edward doesn't like jumping about he is not the age for it, he makes a concession to the party spirit, and to Ah youth youth, he makes this concession in the way that he is sitting on the top stair and not on a chair, but further than this he will not go, he will not be persuaded to move, to rise and flee to some loftier more secret perch where Baldur cannot come.

No, no, Edward will not move, and Baldur with his precise German eye has marked us down, he has said good-bye to little redhead and is coming now and here he is. Well, Baldur did you get a nice partner? Baldur grins with what of *cavaliere servante Don Juan* and *Jakob Casanova* in that smile.

She was very nice, she is but very young, *too young*.

Too young – that is rather . . . is it not? Edward and I are turning this piece over in our mind. *But too young*. That is certainly a pity.

Baldur is a most awful ass. We had him because we wanted to rub up our German. So Baldur came one night to Harriet's flat. And there we were, all set out with pencils and rubbers and exercise books all sitting up like good school-children at Harriet's refectory table. But always it was not being a success. Harriet did not find Baldur at all *simpatisch*. But no. It was a confused evening we had with him.

Reggie and Stephen were also there but I guess we were too frivolous, we did not get the serious angle on study that you must have if you are to have people like Baldur to get anything out of them. Always he was beating his breast like Father Kong to say: 'I am forester.'

Do you do any writing? Do you read much? Do you care for music, have you travelled?

Always came the answer to our conversational inquiries: 'I am forester.' I guess forester in Germany covers a whole hell of a lot, like literae humaniores.

Well look now he was saying, '*Hut* is hat'. But then I said, 'What is Hut?'

'Please? Oh that is also *Hut*.'

'But how extremely confusing and inconvenient, for certainly *I live in my hat* is not the same as *I live in my hut*.'

'Please? Oh that, it does not arise.'

So Harriet took against Baldur, but I was rather fascinated by him, he was such an extremely silly ass but it was interesting, it still is interesting, to see how always he can be just still a little more of a silly ass.

For instance he is very lovey-dovey with women and has always a great success with women and women love him, they just adore those comfortable domestic interiors chez Baldur. 'They come and they come again,' Baldur tells me, 'till perhaps I become tired, I send them off. They are so-o-o nice, for once, for twice for three times, for four times, perhaps, then perhaps it is enough, suddenly they must go.'

'That is sad for them Baldur, you are hard-hearted with these lovesick girls, you are crudèle I can see at once that you are very crudèle.'

He is pleased with this idea, but sentimental too, he plays with the idea of the way he is so *cruel* to these little lovelies. He heaves a sigh.

'Yes, it is sad ah ha' (it is like a hurricane this sigh of this ridiculous Baldur), 'it is sad but they must go.'

He is also a snob. 'I have had girls of the very best families – colonels' daughters.'

'And daughters of the clergy?'

'Yes, certainly, of the very highest families.'

This seducer of the Hochgeborene, he is looking so absurd, he has rolls of little bits of fat the beginnings of the big rolls of fat that will come later. He is such a little silly. I do not for one moment think that he has had all these women and lovely lovesick girls, they exist in his little imagination inflamed by what he would wish to have happened, with his landlady looking the other way.

The only good thing about Baldur is his fondness for his dog, his dog César, his dachshund that accompanied him round and about the forests of Deutschland, travelling incognito in his hunting bag to save the fare on railway journeys, and so staunch and loyal as never to bark.

I am partial to the forests of Deutschland, and even through Baldur's clumsy narrative can come to some idea of them. So this is good. And also I am set for Germany again, to this *Schloss Tilssen* that is cropping up in my life, and must have the speaking practice. So this is good too. So Baldur is good, is at least convenient.

But for Harriet of course she is not set for Germany, so for her he is altogether too boring. But too enervating. But to me he is also in this way diverting as I have said, how much further can he be yet more monstrous and more foolish? Indeed Reader there is no end to it.

Harriet in her elegant green taffeta *robe de style* has come for me now. Running down the stairway standing with my topee at full arms-stretch above my head, I have caught a large pink balloon that is thrown down to me from a high balcony. The party is over.

Several weeks running into months now I have been sick again, I am suffering from the chic Victorian complaint of swooning and the vapours, but I have not yet come to chewing blotting-paper as the anaemic girls of that time did, quires of pink blotting-paper between meals. I imagine them getting together slyly in the rainswept gardens under the rose trees of an evening in July. How many sheets of blotting-paper dear Amelia, well that is good but not so good as Edwina, they say that she . . . whisper, whisper. How very exciting this must have been.

But for me it is sick leave and Lextron and anxiety for my aunt, and for me this vileness of the taste of this drug that comes in all its fiendish taste and expensiveness plus 33⅓ per cent duty from Indianapolis, I have worked it all out it costs one shilling a dose and I must take three doses a day and it is so sick-making that only by thinking of the cost that I have calculated can I keep from being sick.

But I am so glad that I am to have six months' leave ex-office, ex-darling friends, ex-darling and fatiguing parties, ex-poems and book writing, ex-Bottle Green and Freddy. To say good-bye at one swoop to things hated and things loved (work it out for yourself) is a happiness and a turn of fate unlooked for by me. For a fortnight now I have been at an hotel in Josephine's little seaside town in this wreck of a summer that is 1936. Josephine is a darling. I certainly do have good friends. Oh lucky lucky Pompey so savage and so sick and so cross. This fortnight again it has been so wet, so streaming wet with the high gale blowing always down and across the bay and so dangerous it is on the beach, why you stand and look at the cliff – it is this red sandstone cliff – and you look, standing perhaps for safety's sake just at the verge of the sea, between the danger of the land and the danger of the waves that are so tempestuous so stormish so combined with the air and the water to be so completely abandoned and given up to grief and fury in the abandonment of this desperate summertime that lies sobbing tear-wrecked and torn like a beautiful woman that is so desperate she will have her grief and tears, she will have it all out abandoning herself to her fury to what cost of complexion of eyebrightness she does not care or pause to think of for one moment.

I have a sympathetic feeling inside of me for this summer that in this way is like me but you must leave out the beauty because I am not a beautiful woman but only a cross sick Pompey that has this feeling of delicious abandonment to elemental disturbance and this feeling to get away and say the long farewells and to ride away with farewell on her lips for ever. So standing on the sea verge I see the cliffs and suddenly a wedge of cliff detaches itself, oh how furious how wicked in its rage how destructive is this summertime, and slides slowly neatly precisely down the cliffside to engulf with fury and desolation the refreshment hut the bathing huts the kettles within and the primus stoves of the absent tenants. Hurra three times for the engulfing fury of the land and the engulfing fury of the waves.

Josephine is a Christian, she does not have these feelings, so Josephine takes me in the car and we go in to Sway to ride. No Josephine does not ride it gives her a sore behind, but Reine rides on a leading string and I ride off alone. So we tear through the desperate and abandoned New Forest where all is bog and boghole and stumps of trees and all so wet so wet-oh, it is hazardous riding here under the trees and it rains and rains. But when we come to the open heathland it is still blowing this high remote southwesterly gale, and that high wind across the heath excites the horses, they put their ears flat back and dance and long to be off. I do not see why I should ride my horse on a curb, he is a splendid pony and I give him his head I leave the curb slack he goes like the wind. They have long wide rides through the forest but always when we are enjoying it so much hurling ourselves along full out at the gallop I must rein him up and turn back because alas we have lost the riding party. That is a fault. The riding mistress is a nice woman but after I have had several of these exciting rides with her she is getting a little bit cross with me and again I feel creeping over me the disgusting feelings I had as a child at school when they were so cross with me. Why were they so cross with me? It does not matter. I forget. It is always the same, it does not matter. But I was more than cross, I out-Heroded them all, drawing myself with that infuriating ability of childhood into complete aloofness disgust and disdain. They do not put this on the report. They do not put, Is aloof and disdainful. They put, Could do better. But all the time it is this hateful non-co operative feeling indeed it is very aggravating for them. So this riding mistress said to me: 'Why do you ride so long in the stirrup, so slackly, so without taking the bump so like a damned Rookie to ride so flat in this so peculiarly pseudo-military style?' Well I ride flat well I ride flat because I like riding flat and if my horse has an amiable soft trot flat I will ride. But certainly I think now in all fairness to my riding companions of both sexes and many sorts and stations in life it is fortunate for me that I am not dead. I ride so abominably not according to good horsemanship. In Halle I rode there in the riding school, riding round and round at the tail of the docile procession of riding pupils to the sound of Achtung, Achtung, shot at us like a canon ball, but not even this could affright the large placid German mounts or instil into them any desire at all to break the ring, to break from a trot into a canter or, unheard-of luxury, from a canter into a gallop that goes headlong over rough country and takes a girl out of herself. But riding masters and mistresses must think of their horses and to hell with the riders, and if a horse is to get into a full-out slap along god-damned bolt from the blue it's odd chances it will get itself into a sweat and come home with no more rides in it for that day and the little docile pupils queuing up pop-eyed to see the horse that stands panting in its stable with no more rides in it that day for them. So it is nothing for them but to go home and tell mama. Poor horse that must be held and ridden so many times, so many boring times, so many eight-and-sixpences, so much of frustration for that poor horse and long long hours of boredom, and stupid Pompey that frets at every bit and every imaginary bit and curb, so longing to be off, and at the heart of it all, by what untutored premonition, so disliking so dreading this Tilssen-Germany idea that is looming already rather large.

So that already I am forgetting that darling Sir

Phoebus that was my lodestar in a disordered existence, that lodestar of official duties, temperately laid, delightfully pursued, not unsuccessfully carried to what conclusions? (A gloss for this bouquet: How boring, how unfree? . . . How *kind* of him to have me?) I do not concern myself with glosses or conclusions, to me at this moment the pleasure of for once doing what I am told, for once enjoying the luxury of receiving orders, and the delight of play.

Ah, the delight of *play*. Sir Phoebus is at a meeting in the City with the other directors. It is to do with Gold. And the significance of Gold is Dirt. O.K. Mr. Freud. That's the significance of Gold. O.K. my boy, keep it under your hat. But round that Board Room table sit Jew and Gentile, and hostility burns from empire blue eyes to the dark eyes of Israel, lord of the hidden river. And in each separate mind the significance of gold is a separate thing, in the mind of Sir Phoebus a pursuing hunt, a release from the boy's besetting boredom, a hunt a fight a hunt hurra. *L'uomo è cacciatore.* O.K. L'uomo è cacciatore. Keep it under your hat. And in the mind of Empire-Blue-Eyes, the significance of gold is fury and pride and a great beacon of light and power. Blue-eyes looks like he would lay a trail of bullets around the Board Room table.

'We out there', he says, 'have the good of the Colony at heart, *we*' (unpleasantly emphasized – how unpleasant the boy is) '*we* have a reputation to keep up.'

'Pride in their port, defiance in their eye, I see the lords of human kind pass by.' O.K. boy, keep it under your hat, and someday take a look at the trippers on the cross-channel steamers, not, as So-and-So said, on the face of it an imperial people.

And in the eyes of Israel what is the significance of Gold? Unity, flexibility, secrecy, control. Israel has lapped round that course already so many times, so many many times, and his eyelids are a little weary. O.K. Israel, keep it under your hat.

His eyelids are a little weary. This strikes a bell. I shall answer it. Oh Pompey you answer too many bells. Snap out, gentle Reader, I am bell-minded. And one day I know I shall come to no good end. Yea, one day I shall answer the bell and the door will open outwards and I shall find myself in the house of Hades. And inside of the house of Hades all is silent dark and vapourish. Because you will remember what the classical dictionary says about Pluto: None of the goddesses would marry him because his residence was so gloomy. Poor Pluto, so comic-serious now because of Walt's high kicks, but poor poor Pluto, despised and rejected – *Oh Hades, the ladies*. But once inside of the house of

Hades, is there any outcoming? Oh yes, my chicks, for anyone of my name there is passage to and fro, come at will and go at pleasure. But enough of the Casmilus motif, shiftiest of namesakes, most treacherous lecherous and delinquent of Olympians, enough. The very name stinks to heaven, wrapped in whatever concealment of Phoenician Carthaginian double dealing. Avaunt. But always for Pluto I have this soft feeling of gentle pity and suffering. Despised and humiliated by Olympian lovelies, can you blame him if he ran off with the girl from Enna?

There was something sad about the boy, and sweet too, I dare say sweet enough, before he got set up with Minos and Rhadamanthus to judge the souls of all men. And in that gloomy residence, with my abominable namesake in his Punic or Grecian aspect coming uninvited, going unpermitted, conducting on the side a nefarious business to his own advantage, could the boy keep sweet? With what of irritation seething beneath the well bred and polite exterior of the enforced host? 'My dear Hermes-Cas, we are always delighted to see you, of course, there is no need for me to say that. But really sometimes you know (old friends are permitted to be frank) Persephone and I would appreciate a word in advance. At the moment for instance it is perhaps in the slightest way inconvenient. Only in this way my dear fellow, best of friends, most faithful of visitors, only in *this* way, that at this moment we are not able to devote to you the *attention*, to promote and arrange the *entertainment*, your versatility deserves.' Here Pluto would fetch a sigh. 'You see how it is, my hands are so full. The case list grows longer every day. Ah you travellers, you can never know how inimical to hospitality is the legal profession.'

'Never mind about me, dear boy', says Cas, 'I can look after myself' (grim phrase productive of plutonic wince). 'There's a little business connected with Heracles. I'll blow in and see you again later'.

And off goes Cas leaving Pluto to grind his teeth and ponder again the strange uses of kingship, when even within his own realm, on this side of Styx and Phlegethon if you please, the brawling cantankerous buffoonish antics of the god and the hero are to be allowed free rein. Only in the sweet calm eyes of Persephone is there peace and consolation. Sighing again he turns into the Court House, sighing again to think that no rose is without thorn, and even Persephone must have a mother. The ebony portal clangs behind him. It will go hard with the dead to-day.

But to a writer, if not to a judge, the spur of irritation, storming upon occasion the heights of supreme anger, is of the most valuable. And in the life of Pompey at this moment there is indeed plenty to overflowing of this irritation, so that sometimes strolling at evening along the bank of some dear river, scenting the cut grass and the sweet dank riot of mud and weed at the water's edge, I must envy the quiet cow sensuously at chew beneath the elm trees' shade. Ah quiet cow, how come to it. This quietness went before in my experience, is not yet come again, is not to come again for many an exacerbating month in Tilssen beyond Pillau.

It was not long since that I was again in Edinburgh with my Aunt and at dinner with this young professor Dryasdust and his wife. Can the thirties mix with the twenties? I think it already begins to be a little difficult. How aggressive the boy is, how young and how cross. He has a great deal of book knowledge, and outside of books he knows nothing. He is a clever baby, will he ever be anything more, I do not know, in a moment of irritation I guess not. Already the rime of the pedant is upon his young bones. And his pugnacity, the aggressiveness of his prejudice, it is to be heard to be believed. But what has he to offer that one should put up with his abominable manner? Nothing but the derived heartiness of the Belloc and the Beachcomber and the oversimplification of life so dear to the rigid anglo-catholic intellectual. Song at dawn and beer for breakfast, the overblown nevernever-land of *their* south Germany, how sick it makes me feel, already I prefer Berlin.

My thoughts of Munich are not theirs. Just now is Harriet back from Tegernsee. The gross inelegance of the people, the too much of Gemütlickheit, the fat necks and heavy feet turning turning in the dance so clumsily so painstakingly wrong, wrong.

'They dance for their health,' says the young Baron to Harriet. 'They are very lowclass these people, the Bavarians have the backsides of peasants and the brains of the pig.'

Oh ho, Baron, but you tip the scales at the other side, so slim so small so carefully correct and in such a blue funk is the dear boy that to protect himself from Nazi accusations of incorrect thinking he has joined the Army. What desperate remedy. And now he must leave his address and wherever he goes, tripping off light of foot to each fresh resort, he is followed by official telegrams growing steadily in tonal discourtesy and menace. And beneath the Gemütlichkeit and the health-dance and the papa-love-baby there is all of this menace and the memory always of the Nazi martyr memorial in Munich where two sentries stand night and day and the passer-by must salute. Yes but he must salute, papa, mama, baby, they must raise the hand and make the absurd and revolting spectacle of a fascist discipline. Or they can cross the road and pass by unsaluting, unmolested. But to do this too often, is not this rather dangerous, is it not the thin end of the wedge of the beginning of incorrect thinking?

When I am walking with the wife of the professor Dryasdust we are getting along well enough. But when we turn back to dinner and he is there it is all very extremely painfully, not so good at all. Don't you dare to put Paracelsus in your book, he shouts at me, blue eyes hot in hot face. And why should I not put Paracelsus in my book, have you made a corner in Paracelsus, is Paracelsus now and forever to be your speciality, *spécialité de chez Dryasdust?* I won't have it, he screams. Then I shall put him in at once. I shout at him, he shouts at me, his wife falls sulky-silent, regarding the vegetable dishes, regarding the french beans fried in vinegar and butter by Bavarian cookie who is also rather cross and pounding in and out to shout cross Bavarian dialect at the English nuisances.

Ah this is a very painful situation now, and for once I am becoming I am really beginning to feel a little – well it is for instance embarrassing is it not. Girlie Dryasdust comes out of her vegetable reverie to say with biting precision to her husband something that is so bitingly precise it should not be said to husbands in front of helpless guest. How much money have you got in the Bank? Crescendo of anger and affront: We are living beyond our income. Oh return to the vegetable reverie dear Mrs. Dryasdust, no alas never can the vegetable reverie if returned to be quite what it was before, so happy, so quiet, so inconspicuous, leaving to the professor and myself the onus of the quarrel. I am appalled, perhaps they are going to have a fight. I think now I am a little sorry for the sweet boy, I have no doubt at all that his wife is . . . well is she not? Oh peinliches Situation. I draw his fire again upon myself. Why for instance, I say, are you so furious with me, why are you this cross-dog that cannot speak for fury and whose countenance changes so often from the pale to the extremely red it is like Stratford Canning when the Turks in council with him begged him to control the choler that too faithfully drove the blood to his face for all to note? Is it perhaps because you wish yourself to write? Me? roars Dryasdust, I am writing a thesis on Paracelsus. Now by this time we are up from the table and sitting around. So Dryasdust takes down a volume of Pater and this is to show me that this indeed is prose that I could not have known. It is a pity I could not have known before, but you see it is a pity, but here is my chance here is my chance now to learn for the first time, if indeed it is not already too late. He sighs, takes his pipe from his mouth and reads. And reads. Oh but it is dreadful. Now this is what I cannot bear to support for one moment longer. The too-ripeness, the concealed verse forms, the succulent young voice of the insufferably teaching young professor, the falling back of the ten years since I read Pater, the too familiar and infuriating intrinsic cadences, the dying fall at the end of each paragraph. And the eyelids are a little weary . . . The return of the pagan world, the sins of the Borgias . . . And tinged the eyelids and the hands. Darling, I say, turning to his wife, I cannot support this. Pussy not feel well. I collect my hat, my gloves. I think of the most impossible unguestly things to say. I do not say them. Here the thirties are at a disadvantage. We think but cannot say. They say but cannot think. I think: Yes at twenty one may read Pater – but not aloud to friends, not that, never that, at twenty it is even commendable to read Pater, it shows that at least one has an ear for the less subtle harmonies of English prose. At twenty I could, but I hope did not, quote just that passage, but without the book. Here I am getting a little superior. In my moment of wicked crossness and superiority I think again of his essay on Paracelsus, and I think, but do not say: there is another quotation that will I think fit that very well, oh very well indeed. It is by a greater than Pater. And I think and I laugh and I think: To win the applause of schoolboys and furnish matter for a prize essay. Good-bye, now, I must go, I say. I have on my hat and gloves. I go, they come with me to my hotel. I glance at the clock. It is nine. So with all my forbearance the greatest insult is upon my side. It is 9 o'clock in the evening.

So sitting in my room at the office thinking of Sir Baronet at his meeting in the City 'to do with Gold' and of Empire-Blue-Eyes in his lust for pride and power and of Israel of the weary eyelids, this bell has been rung, and how sad I am that this beastly Pompey must always give way to such crossness, such sudden rage, and ferocity to be so irritable, irritated so easily by the stupid irritability of Dryasdust that she must go home at 9 o'clock to darling Auntie Lion, who has about her too the power of anger upon occasion, but not this nervous irritability that has in it the pulse of our time. For we have in us the pulse of history and our times have been upon the rack of war. And are, and are. And I have read in the memoirs of Van Weyden that not the least part of the torture of the rack is the succeeding torment of the nerves newly released from its physical reality to continue that torment unpressed and undesired, for the undoing of their victim. So it is with us, and lucky indeed those in close immediate touch with an older calmer undriven generation, a father, a mother, a Lion of

Hull, to draw from them at need upon their strength.

Oh I do love my Aunt and so much I admire her. She is so reasonable, so balanced, so sound, and yet so kind and practical, and she never reads dotty novelettes like a lot of ladies do. And what does she read? Well, this is again a source of profound admiration and perpetual wonder to me. Well what she reads is the Blue Book on India and the County Cricket scores.

Very interested and au fait with India is the Lion of Hull, and so sensible in her pronouncements, why the Viceroy himself might do worse. For she sways neither to the sentimentalism of the pseudo-Kipling tea-planter who alone in India now, aping his betters, the army of a long-past generation, cries: Shoot first, and not veering either to a sentimentalism that will cry: Abdicate, evacuate, India for the Indians, a something perhaps that must not come to pass yet for a long time. For no more than this darling Mrs. Dryasdust having expressed her appalling sentiments can thereafter retire again into a vegetable reverie, so cannot England, with 200 years of conquest and government behind her, hand over to Indians an India that for better or for worse can never be again.

But my Aunt can tell you how many dialects there are extant in All India, and how the Government is to cope with the problems they have themselves created of an English-educated middle class with so little of outlet for its English education, and she can have a very real sympathy for this poor government that certainly has its hands full of the pricks of a nettle bunch it has so eagerly plucked.

And she also likes books on military campaigns and soldiers' memoirs. She likes those admirable snorty books by Mr. Fortescue and she likes Francis Younghusband's *The Relief of Chitral*.

(And this comes to me with the thought that I must buy her another copy, for I left hers in a rabbit hole in the Monk's Green Woods, to be out of the rain, and could not find it again.)

But my Aunt is a purist in the matter of Indian situations, for she will not read a novel upon the theme, in case it is too full of elaborate fancies and Stuff and Nonsense. Stuff and Nonsense are the twin bogies of my Aunt's existence, and really I think this is full of high courage, this way that she will tilt against the windmills of stuff and nonsense. She is an inverted Quixote in an age when it is fashionable for every windmill to pretend to be something that is not a windmill.

When I am in St. Paul's Cathedral I identify my Aunt with the memorial tablets that are hung there; they are so English high-nosed 18th century damn-your-eyes, I do so love them. They are different from our mawkish tablets of to-day. Always they are soldiers' tablets. They are young men or old men. They sometimes have a statue to show General So-and-So. It is a pity, he got shot amidriff, he is tumbling off his charger, that is somehow never looking in the least like an English charger, but has always about him the wild and untidy look of a horse with its long mane flowing upon the breeze of a Greek relief.

And always on the tablet you may read that these gentlemen, the young and the old, fell in battle for their country. Just that, do you see? Did they Make the great Sacrifice? They did not. They fell in battle for their country.

But what, the tendentious foreigner will ask, had their country to do with places so far afield as Corunna, Quebec, Pondicherry and other far-off famous occasions?

And about this we have long discussions at breakfast because we do not so much like the peace-at-any-price people who go about to-day to apologize for England and to pretend that she hasn't really got so much of the earth's surface, it only looks that way on these jingo maps. Because we do not like this, yes, it smacks a little of stuff and nonsense and also a little of hypocrisy. For if we are not nowadays the conquerors and pioneers, we are at least the beneficiaries under empire, and at least and basest we have cheap sugar.

Oh certainly I hate the excuses and the propaganda and the share-juggling that are a part of war conquest, but our hands have not been clean of this in the past, and the parsons who write to the papers to say that England holds commission from heaven to colonize the earth, must surely be dottily overlooking the Jameson Raid and the Rand Kaffir business and even the splendid mendaciousness and begum-baiting of perpetually hard-up Clive and Hastings.

Thank God the executive government and the permanent officials bandy about no such excuses or explanations, dealing preferably and competently with the fait accompli and devoting their energies to the nipping of opposition in the first green bud and to the promotion of good plumbing.

We hold commission from heaven neither to colonize nor decolonize. It is not heaven's business at all, except perhaps in this way, if you care to think of it in this way, that England colonizes because she is a colonizing animal, and heaven, if you like to hand it to heaven or to God, is the creator of all animals good and bad, colonizing or otherwise.

But England is also a very cunning animal, very suave and astute indeed, and, in only supplying a demand that she sensed when first it came into the wind of modern humanitarianism, has thought up a lot of excuses for her âme intime de colonisateur. But these are to make you smile and turn away, they are not to be taken seriously except by smarty-clever babies like Professor Dryasdust who has on his mantelpiece, *pour épater* Pompey, Lord Mottistone and Sir Samuel Hoare, a picture postcard issued by the Italian bureau de propaganda to show a good Italian soldier striking the slave-chains off the wrists of a kneeling Abyssinian. But is not this the very most harmless and elementary form of propaganda?

When England plays that game she can play it better than that, more thoroughly more vilely more unanswerably final.

My thoughts turn sadly to Casement and the astuteness of the at that moment of time necessary defamation of his character by the circulation of his diary. Ah ha, my little Professor, there is propaganda in excelsis with the imprimatur of the British Government upon it. Must the Belgians be held to opprobrium at that fatal minute of history, with 1914 on the time sheet and the necessity of presenting to a public of military age the spectacle of la petite Belgique outraged and debauched by the advancing Pruss? *Violée tant que jamais*, how is that? Oh that is so-o-o good, why it is quite excellent. The men spring to arms. But if the sacrificial victim be not so pure, so immaculate, will that serve so well? It will not. Jeune fille avec tache, violée tant que jamais. That is perhaps something to make you laugh. And fight? Oh no, we are not fighting to-day, thank you so much.

Do you see? — How clever, how abominably necessary the discrediting of all that Casement in his white heat of indignation, and a little of stuff and nonsense too, had accomplished? Before the war his name stood high, his word was taken, the opprobrium of the world fell upon Belg um in her African misconduct. But alas, dear Casement, the times are against you, it is August 1914, it is later than that, already the sparks are set to a general conflagration, you must go.

I understand the motives of my country. It is better than to excuse or deny. That she is astute and upon occasion equivocal, I believe. That she has conquered in greed, held in tenacity, explained in casuistry, I agree. But fools asking foolish questions have nothing to expect but folly or casuistry. And here for folly is the Commission from Heaven, and here for casuistry the Sole Good of the Resident Population. And beneath both, there is a modicum of mishandled truth. Such, as I have shown, is the âme intime de colonisateur, and such again is the good of the native population, that is not the whole and sole consideration but a substantial part consideration, resting, again at basest, upon the convenience of the army of occupation, upon the ease and economy of public services. No empire has ever long survived a too savage oppression of subject peoples. 'One must be friendly', as a certain great actress of my acquaintance said, confronted at Frinton by children of divorce on both sides of her family, and by their co-responding papas and mamas. One must be friendly.

Yes, it is of practical convenience to be friendly, in private as in public life. Regulate either upon a man-made theory, however fascinating in the taprooms and colleges, and so sure as I am writing this sitting quietly in my room at 6.45 p.m., There will be trouble.

In case that you may now be getting bored with Pompey, and to make a nice break and a 'change' for you, dear Reader, I will give you a long long extract from one of these military memoirs to which Aunty Lion and I are so partial. To my mind it illustrates and emphasizes what I have been saying, but if you do not think so, you will at least I hope find it not without an intrinsic interest to make you write to me to give you the name of the book to go out and buy it to read yourself.

For you may, for all I know, be like that sweet boy Karl I had so many years ago in your hatred of excerpts, anthologies and all of that etcetera.

Ethical imperialism. (Yes, on the whole I am afraid this Memoirist is more ethical than military.) 'We must never forget for a moment in our struggle against England that the British Empire is held together by its prestige as much as by its sea communications . . . The foundations of British imperialism reach back into the dim past and are no longer called in question by the public opinion of the world . . . England had a better name in the world than we . . . She stood in our way everywhere. The eminent service rendered by the enterprise of individual Germans must not blind us to this fact. They were not acting, as the Englishmen were, as representatives of a national ethos . . . England has never founded her claims in the world on the fortune of war alone. She has always convinced the world that England's power serves justice and freedom, only so would the world tolerate and even abet an island people of 45 millions bringing the best portions of the earth under its sway. Two factors have played a decisive part in forming this world opinion. When England went forth to prey she always preserved her world conscience in opposition.' The writer says now that when this preying animal that is England is at a moment lost in the ecstasy of her own aggression, marauding at this moment perhaps too openly, too barefacedly, for the world's stomach, in an orgy of annexation, divested for once (in this fine careless moment) of the good Cloak *Peaceful-Penetration*, (most becoming of uniforms for the *âme intime de colonisateur*), she will yet preserve in her midst 'men and groups who are potential holders of power . . . who have always protested loudly as the representatives of a better England, and fought and suffered for their conviction. These representatives of the better England often come to power subsequently and heal the wounds which the British sword has dealt. Thus Campbell-Bannerman made a moral conquest of the Transvaal, against whose forcible conquest he had for years been foremost in protesting. And so it comes about that England weakens the world's moral power of resistance to her deeds of violence by making it possible for the world to say that England's victims will in the end become reconciled to English sway and even happy under it.

England's great political programme, had it stood alone, would not have created this world opinion. She needed and produced a large number of administrators whose character and whose daily conduct of affairs embodied the English principle that the happiness and the rights of other people were a part of England's national purpose. Lord Cromer took Egypt's part as only a man who loved the country for its own sake could do. In the last Armenian massacre Major Doughty Wylie saved the lives of thousands of Armenians at the risk of his own life by the mere authority of the British uniform . . . During our' (the speaker is still our honey-tongued Enemy) 'during our victorious offensive, Haig's telegram: 'They have broken through our system of defences' makes a terrible impression. Haig himself asks for a generalissimo. The British strike is called off. Ramsay MacDonald joins the Lords of the Battle Cry. With Haig's telegram begins a period of that heroic truthfulness of which England in misfortune has often proved herself capable, to the detriment of her enemies . . . the prevailing tone is still one of dour determination to look the facts in the face.'

My excerpt closes with his comments upon the Press: 'With some notable exceptions the German press in matters of foreign policy is a hurly burly of opinions expressed by ill-informed editors. The great British Newspapers' (with which I fear he confounds the *Daily Yell*) 'not only reflect important decisions affecting war policy, they also prepare them. The Cabinet and the War Office are often at loggerheads; both look for backing in the Press . . . It is true that

Britain is now our toughest and most powerful foe, and holds the whole alliance together . . . If the British people is shown victory, victory it will have at any price, and the idea of a peace of compromise will be rejected with indignation and with all the endurance of the British character. True there are still serious hitches in the British war machine; but it goes; and if it stops the fire can always be stoked with Cavell and Fryatt incidents and wave after wave of patriotic fury released.' The Prince's metaphor is a little mixed, but it is notorious that Germany seldom denied herself the pleasure of pouring coals upon the waves.

Out of this medley of translation, gloss and excerpt you, my pursuing Reader, may for yourself distinguish the elements of flattering, very flattering envy hysteria, melodrama and sense.

But how is our Colonizing Animal, our so darling pet Lion of these British Isles? How now does he find himself? Well chaps, he is by this time sleek as a cat with the cream of this unction. 'Yes', I can hear him say, viewing himself with complacency through the eyes of our Memoirist, 'undoubtedly that is me. Sophisticated girls like Pompey Casmilus that must go to being so-o-o smart can have their cheap chat about native instincts and âme whatever-it-is. But this German Princeling, he is the boy for me. Machiavelli-cum-what was it he said? All thought out beforehand and mapped to the merest inch. Instinct my foot.' And the insufferable darling animal will turn over on his sleek fat belly and have a good sleep – with the poets, I hope, to trouble his dreams with the prods and pains he at times so richly deserves.

> When God commanded this hand to write
> In the studious hours of black midnight
> He told me that all I wrote should prove
> The bane of all that on earth I love.

There is a nervous irritation in this book and a tide in the affairs of Pompey which taken at the flood leads – God knows where.

One part of my multifarious and absorbing duties at the office is the reading of manuscripts from presumptive authors. A phrase culled from one of these manuscripts, editorially rejected, is appropriate to my present mood. 'There was about him a subtle suggestion of jumpiness.' So there is about Pompey this fascinating aura. A long narrow head, (I picture my contributor's model), a twitchy manner and just about him too that something that also suggests he will very shortly leave the country for an indefinite period by an inconspicuous port for no known destination. Do you see?

I am involved in the proof corrections of my first novel, even while I write these words, so well on now into the second. Perhaps it is a little debilitating to begin a second while the first is on hand? It is as if a nursing mother should at once start another baby – a thing which we advise our readers on no account to do. 'Send me a stamped addressed envelope, little wife, and I will write to you in more detail.' For remember, darling, prevention is better than abortion.

But for me it is neither prevention nor abortion but full steam ahead under some feeling of desperation, for some *rather* distant seas of *rather* northerly aspect and cold, cold, cold.

I am already sick of my first book, I must have read it through by now at least half a dozen times. It is enough. But also I have now to think of these three hundred poems that must be retyped selected and discarded, and that thought bores me so awfully. No really it is too much. It is lovely quickly to write a poem and then quickly it is finished, it is all over and to be forgotten. But alas it is not. For now with the passage of a good many years, oh yes a *good* many years, there are already these so many pieces of paper and backs of envelopes and this litter of paper – Oh the mechanics of authorship are frightful. I have now got this litter-phobia very strongly developed, this detestation of little bits of paper and the frightfully boring job-job-job of arranging and selecting and discarding, and arranging (this was a supreme achievement) in alphabetical order of first lines.

Do you see, dear Reader, the cold feet I am getting, and the feeling as I read through these rather disturbing rather unquiet rather hateful poems that I had better quit writer quit or prove the bane of all that on earth I love? It is a neurosis and to be resisted, of course, it is to be resisted and not given way to for one moment, *Danton, no stuff and nonsense!* Up, the Lion!

Did this Aunty Lion for instance, did she not have troubles of her own, and all of this older generation that you have written of so smugly as if to say they never had cause to bat an eyelid that lived through as many wars as us moderns in our vanity of excusing?

But yes I cannot think of the answer to that sturdy argument which I seem to have read laid out forcibly by the critic I saw at the party – Mr. So-and-So from Guess-Where.

But yes, no, all I can think to say is, Oh but the radio and oh but the electric drills and oh but the underground railway and oh but the . . . Yes, it is nothing but the temporary under-par-ness of the sad Pompey that is getting a bit off the handle these days.

So now I will tell about the afternoon I spent with my proof-correcting. You must imagine a very *very* hot afternoon. Oh but it is so hot you cannot breathe. And also I have chosen this very hot weather to have an attack of influenza. So I am just on my feet again but feeling rather sick and not very kind and docile at all. So there is the man there who is to help me through this ordeal. It is sad for him, indeed I am sorry. But all the time I am there, it is an enormous room, very elegant very long and lofty, but somehow it is not very easy to breathe. So all the time further to distract and irritate us there are messages coming through from Sir Phoebus.

But there is the message from his lady aunt to say to remind him to buy some smoked cod's roe. But I have tried, I say, I have rung up Fortnum's and Harrods, and cookie has rung up Selfridge's, it is absolutely not the season for smoked cod's roe, it is but absolutely impossible. For instance it is possible to force asparagus out of season, but the female cod will not be so constrained. She will not have it. It is impossible.

And there is the message from my uncle, that Lord Snooks wants to know how much bloody well longer he is to hold on to Korpsdorf Prefs. And then I must think very carefully and cleverly, Now what were Korpsdorf Prefs. this morning? And last week? And so there is a possibility that they will shoot higher? Oh yes, I certainly think they will touch two and seven-eighths, so it is perhaps worth holding on, and holding on till the cows come home? Because really Lord Snooks holds a packet and if he starts to unload – no that must be prevented. My Uncle Stockbroker says so.

So I come back to my proofs in rather a scattered frame of mind. And here before me on the page is another problem: Was Semele the aunt or the sister of Pentheus? But how abominable I have been, how frightful, how could I have left this important relationship-question to the chance of my mendacious memory? But this is a point of the utmost urgent importance. But it is already running round in my mind with Lord Snooks and his Korpsdorf Prefs. And it is running round with the offended female cod that must not, must not be thought of to be mishandled in this out of season way. It is an outrage even to think of this quiet female cod – Well now look, she is sitting at rest upon the lovely soft warm green mud of some steep rock pool. And do I not wish that I was so happily situated as she? I do wish this.

Oh it is so hot. And I am feeling so distraught I cannot breathe and I keep looking round and thinking: Oh if we could only have the window open. Oh if only there was no window at all. Oh if we could only have the window open. And I say: Oh if I could have a cigarette.

But there are no cigarettes, and I guess this is God getting back at Pompey for the frightful floater I made the other day when talking and walking with chère Harriet. Oh darling, I say, looking at my open cigarette case, oh I am so sorry that I cannot offer you a cigarette but I only have one.

Oh how very unlike Christ and Sir Philip Sidney and even St. Whatshisname that at least split the cloak-cigarette in two. Oh but how frightful. But it was unconscious.

Well Miss Casmilus, I don't think much of your unconscious if that is the sort of fantasia it puts up in a tight corner. So now you see there are no cigarettes and that is something for once you get that you deserve.

Yea, frightful Pompey, I guess that will larn you to be a toad.

Oh when I see Harriet next I will remember to give her a packet of Players. Now please to remember that, and already your path is beginning to be strewn with Reliefs of Chitral and Players cigarettes, for a something to make up for the something that is so frightful in your conduct.

But is there not a little faint glimmer of false dawn hope shining over in the east of my night sky, if I can remember to remember about this at a moment like this?

I smile suddenly upon my fellow worker. Let me see, where are we now? Why we have done another twenty pages, by God we have.

Oh do you think, I say, that we could send out for cigarettes?

Well, it is for a full twenty pages of 'is there a life beyond the gravy' type of type-slip, to say nothing of misspellings in five languages and misquotations, and heavily sub-surface libel actions, that I have said nothing. So surely now at last I may say: *Can we not send out for some cigarettes?*

So then I go to sit over by the window that my fellow worker has opened up for me.

I guess I am a cross for him to bear. But if there were for instance to be no crosses to bear, how acquire merit? So I look out of this beautiful wide open window and my fellow worker goes to get me a glass of water.

But oh, there is yet one more *frightfulness* for me to have this hot hot afternoon. For there on the iron balcony lies a dead bird. But it is something that is so horrible, so sad. It is a bird that has fallen out of its eggshell, it lies there splosh on the iron ledge, it has absolutely no feathers on at all. But no feathers – that is horrible. For a bird, that is not possible. But is it my fault? Did I ask that the bird should fall out of its eggshell? To lie untimely upon the balcony? Without a feather upon it? An *embryo*?

Oh now do you see how frightful the mechanics of authorship are when one is involved at once in so many disturbances and cannot keep that peace and integrity of the inner life of the soul that is for the whole health and strength of body and mind?

So I got sick of it, sick at heart with a great world pain, and sick of the sight of page proofs and sick of the irritation of a stimulated imagination that must go to having so many thoughts, so many many thoughts.

And I become quite set to death. And I think of the weekend I spent with my sister Mary at Felixstowe Ferry when it was so quiet, so very quiet and lovely. We went on the river Deben, in a dinghy, rowing at night-time upon the dark and phosphorescent waters.

And now I sit down to write a poem, to set out the peace of that river, and the way I am longing for it, and the search for peace that is only to be found perhaps in death. So I write:

All the waters of the river Deben
Go over my head to the last wave even
Such a death were sweet to seven times seven.

Death sits in the boat with me
His face is shrouded but he smiles I see
The time is not yet, he will not come so readily.

But he smiles and I smile it is pleasant in the boat
    at night
There is no moon rising but from the east a light
Shines in the sky is it dawn or dawn's twilight?

Over here the waters are dark as a deep chasm
Shadowed by cliffs of volcanic spasm.
So dark so dark is the waves' fashion

But the oars dip I am rowing they dip and scatter
The phosphorescence in a sudden spatter
Of light that is more actual than a piece of matter.

Up the Deben we row I row towards Waldringfield
It is a long way yet, my arms ache but will not yield
In this physical tiredness there is a happy shield.

Oh happy Deben, oh happy night and night's
companion Death
What exultation what ecstasy is in thy breath
It is as salt as the salt silt that lies beneath.

Flow tidal river flow, draw wind from the east,
Smile pleasant Death, smile Death in Darkness blest,
But tarry day upon the crack of dawn; thou comest
unwisht.

Hurra, already I am feeling quieter in my head and the evening is cooler. I imagine myself lying quietly in Freddy's arms – if only Freddy were not quite so emphatically Freddy but perhaps a little of the chimera I fell in love with, that sweet shape that has vanished from my eyes. Eheu Chimera, I will track you down yet, I will hunt you to earth in some green forest of Deutschland, be sure that you shall not escape me.

My aunt is cutting up bacon rind for our birds. She is doing this with rather a shaky hand, in half an hour the taxi will be here and I must say good-bye. The shadow of farewells is upon the bacon rind and to-day the birds will not have such a finely chopped feast as yesterday. We take the rind and the breakfast crumbs and the crusts broken into pieces and put them on the lawn; now we stand back behind the window curtains and watch for cats. My aunt will have no cat in our garden. Also my aunt will see fair play between the birds, who sitting now and swinging gently upon the tree branches are about to have this lovely meal-o of bacon rind and crusty bread. It is a sunny day and early in the morning, the grass is heavy with dew and the sun low upon our neighbours' roofs.

Yesterday the gardener was here, and now the garden, newly prinked and tidied, the paths as neat and formal as a parade, shines beneath this early morning sun that has broken through to break the rain and storm clouds of past months. How very spry the garden looks, like a good child that has a washed face and a clean pinafore.

My aunt taps sharply on the window from behind the curtain. The thrush is cheating. Thrusting the smaller sparrows aside with greedy beak he gobbles up the lovely rind. Now, now, says my aunt. Now, now. That will do.

The birds scatter for the moment but again alight. There is a young sparrow that is so fat he must surely come to bursting but still he is being fed. Yes, is it not absurd? His parent birds, thin and worn with this unequal task, press ever more and more rind crumb and crust upon the greedy offspring who, between mouthfuls that would become a pelican, can only gobble-gobble-cluck-cluck for more ever more meal-o.

But now the great black cat is upon the fence, tensed to spring.

Oh hateful cat with green deceitful eyes, coming up early in the morning from what ramshackle night of love. Away most unsympathetic of animals, away marauder.

I run out into the garden, shouting as I run. He regards me with malevolent eye, he is so furious. And so suddenly, what use is it to be furious? He can do nothing but slink away, landing with soft thud upon our neighbour's flower bed. There falling in with low company, his own companions of the midnight hour, he can for the moment absorb himself in their delinquent antics, birdless and breakfastless upon the call of love.

Farewell, farewell, saddest and sweetest of words, this is the morning of my farewell. For I am to meet Josephine at Victoria and our journey is set to that ominous Tilssen that is beyond Pillau and for me beyond thought.

Already the strain of the unknown journey is upon me and the anxiety of the passage through time and space.

For if to-day is now eight o'clock in this darling England, to-morrow will be eight o'clock getting towards Berlin; and the next day eight o'clock further east and northwards, to a destination that shall be for me the 'change' the doctors (how willing to forgo the burden of my recovery) have stipulated.

'You must have a complete change of scene. And a long rest. Far from towns. Near the sea. Close to the best medical opinion. If possible with pine-woods in the vicinity.' 'And a Kurhaus?' 'Yes, certainly a Kurhaus, if that is convenient. But rest is obligatory and sleep and a sea voyage,' says the doctor, getting rather wild in the head to remember at once everything that is necessary to a completely successful cure. 'And congenial companions?' I am helping him out. 'Yes, certainly,' he says, adding in some bathos of desperation and reiteration, 'and a complete change away from everything.' Away from everything? Aha. So. I think we have found the spot, this Schloss Tilssen of dear Josephine's choice is getting rather important for English invalids. A friend of Josephine's stayed there at some crisis in her life, so frightful and so vividly depicted by Josephine of the inspired tongue, that now only the *general* impression of a *general* calamity miraculously averted by the good agency of Tilssen air and Tilssen comfort remains with me.

That is perhaps as well for you, gentle Reader, as Josephine's tales remembered and retold in detail would delay our arrival at Tilssen by some further two or three volumes of Pompey's reminiscences.

Yesterday was my last day in my room at the office for it is to be six months. Sir Phoebus has given me a bottle of Floris's 127 *Bouquet* scent for a combined birthday and good-bye present. And with so much of kindness and understanding and encouragement he has wished me better.

'Don't get up to tricks, take care of yourself and come back with some drawing-room wisecracks for my funny speeches in the autumn,' he says.

I have answered the last of the letters, I have dealt with the last of the dividends, losing myself in patient and delightful absorption in this fascinating arithmetic of the four-and-sixpence in the pound income tax deduction, upon fractional holdings of gross allotments, affording me the ever pleasing opportunity of using once again the baronet-taught long division by the Italian method.

Dear Reader, work *this* out for yourself. You multiply and subtract in the same line, by the dual operation decreasing labour and increasing liability to error.

How I adore doing this. But it is completely to forget the pressure of other-way thought. It is a delight, and an absorption, and an escape. I am not sure at all that perpetual long division by the Italian method would not prove as salutary (and so much more convenient to my friends and my employer) as this hazardous Tilssen démarche.

Lord Victor Moan, bowing himself above me, has said:

'I hope Miss Casmilus that you will make a complete recovery.'

He raises his hat to me for the last time for six months.

It is over. How kind everybody is in this office, how kind and more than kind. You would think that the Company had been founded, nourished and brought to its present 15 per cent dividend-paying perfection for this sole purpose, to wish this tiresome Pompey again to good health and to give her six months to run free of boring duty. How kind. But it is over. Farewell, everlasting farewells. Farewell a long farewell to all my weakness that has brought me to this point of being so enervating so exasperaing and so farouche.

From Berlin we go to Swinemünde and take ship from there. Steaming slowly along the too familiar too boring coast of the Baltic Sea, the faces of my darling friends in their farewell group on the platform at Victoria are still before me. Dearest of all my sister Mary and my aunt. So anxious for me, but I shall come back, why certainly I shall come back to them, my one secure hold, my anchorage in this world of stormy seas, how could I not indeed come back to them, tried a hundred times, faithful and excusing in the most desperate of my sadness. Indeed, coldly sadly anxiously watching the coastline slipping slipping further and further to the westward of us how great a sense of foreboding I have and a nostalgie for their quiet home and darling England. But the coastline slips away into the sunset, and the ship ploughs on towards distant Pillau and beyond that and again beyond. This is an almost tideless sea, but the waves are heavy, swelling up sullenly beneath our boat to rock it with a rather savage intent as much as to say: Wait.

There is a time, one may be with a friend, with a very dear friend, it makes no difference, when loneliness and the fear that waits upon it strikes at the physical heart, so that there is a pain that is physical with the physical pain of a very extreme icy coldness. And the power of speech departs though there was never a greater desire for speech, however banal, and never a greater desire to watch in friendliness the face of some familiar friend. But between yourself and this desire, craven or childish in tune with your mood and judgment, strike down like a thunder stroke the words of Chaucer: Here is but wildernesse. Oh death could not be more cold. And this coldness of this loneliness and fear carries with it its own most searching pang, the burden of a prophecy: I am your future. So that even the relief of death appears a vain thing, and life-in-death our sole whole scope and penalty.

In *Parsifal* the aged Titurel has died, but through the mercy of the Saviour (viewpoints on the Saviour it should be remembered are as variable as the minds of men) continues to live in the grave. Titurel appears to attach great value to this glum circumstance, and cries from the serecloths 'By the grace of the Saviour I live in the tomb.' To each man his fancy, but this is not mine. Yet in these sad moments into the grave we go and whether we enjoy it or not such is our experience. To die and not to die, to go into the cold earth of our own sadness, there to wait as best we may the relief of happier thoughts upon a thought that shall drive away all memory of pain.

O silent visitation
In negation of all presences
O felicity of the imagination
O merit
Of integrity in solitude
Where was born the desolation
Of this night sky that lightly lightly
Treads upon the desert
In patience lost beyond cognizance
O desolate night sky
O profundity of patience
Bearing lightly lightly
Upon the desert of the time track
O behold in silence
The shapes of the prevision
That dance and turn again
From comprehension
I am waiting for you.

So that with Josephine I am a little cold and aloof, a little ominous too in my feelings, for this coldness is not such a good augury for our time together indeed I fear it may go hard with us. But by and by she will talk, and like a vampire that has learnt the secrets of the grave (oh shut up, Dryasdust) I shall batten upon the stream of her confidences, for there never was anything so full of the life of everyday, of the warmth and cosiness and smell of homo sapiens as these confidences of chère Josephine, who is but now, unfortunately, wrapped in her own night of foreboding for the comfort and cleanliness of our cabins. When we came on board it was rather amusing, really rather thrilling in the way that these journey-breaks are. By steamer, by train and now by steamer again, we are well on our way, almost our destination is at hand – almost. But I glance again at the boring flat coastlines, the lights of the tiny Ost-See bathing places, I can in my imagination see the beachbaskets, the sand walls surrounding them, the striped umbrellas and the notices stuck along the sand dunes: Beyond the waves is danger to life. Lebensgefahr. And beyond Pillau, beyond our journey's end, is there there also perhaps Lebensgefahr in the form of immense breakers rolling up again upon the sea of thought, for me for her for the baby Reine? I could wring my hands really that I have thus weakly allowed myself to be sent over the seas, for I never before had such a desire to be in England and upon our own immeasurably superior seaboard. But *there* the tides come and go upon wide beaches and *there* is a vast space for happy play at low tide on the sands or rocks, to fish paddle paddle-bathe (I am thinking of our somewhat evasive north sea at Saltfleet,

Lincs, which this morning is in England and tomorrow across to the continent). And there at Saltfleet are the most grand and enormous sand dunes and vast cavities behind, ramparts and bastions of sand, grass tufted to stand against the open seawinds. And there are salt sea marshes with the sea seeping up beneath the samphire beds, and there as a young child I stayed with my family. And what was the first thing that Pompey did, arriving there with her young sister Mary? Well the first thing that Pompey and Mary did was to go running running away from mama and Auntie Lion away out and across the salt marshes and sand dunes to get completely lost beyond the wide and treacherous river that flowed between our hired cottage and the seaboard, to cost mama and Aunt what of time thought trouble desperation affright and indignation in our ultimate recovery, which was I hope accompanied by a 'good smack'.

Or I would like to be again upon the Deben at Felixstowe Ferry. To play about all day and through the night, being ramshackle in the mud, in a little sailing boat, to shift the sail and take to oars, to be ramshackle in a creek. Oh that is for me the highest pleasure.

But here I am, for good or bad, set again to foreign parts. The very foreign parts, it comes to me now, that Auntie Lion as a young girl of fifteen or so explored many a time with my grandfather sailing his own extremely beastly and smelly little outboard-engined sailing boat along from Hull, Eng. to of all unlikely destinations, distant and by association ludicrous – Riga. Whether my aunt was shanghaied by my maternal grandfather or duty-driven I do not know. But only I do know that her detestation for foreign parts is only equalled by her detestation for marine travel by whatever medium, from dinghy with sail ahoist to lady liner of immense tonnage. Duty or Shanghai tactics drove her aboard but neither the one nor the other could force her ashore. So that when I use the word explore I am misleading. My grandfather explored, his daughter, casting inimical and insular eyes upon the seaview of Riga, stayed aboard, preferring the accustomed discomfort of a marine existence to the unknown detestability of Muscovy. And my grandfather, I like to think, had an uneasy conscience to bring him back after short absence to this decisive daughter who at fifteen ruled his house and servants and ordered his life.

Well we are not at Riga yet, but in my memory there is Horstseebad, Rugenwalde, Stolpmünde, Danziger Bucht, Pillau, Cranz and all of the Seedienst Ostpreussen to give us the feeling that we are getting on.

The first thing we did after leaving Swinemünde was this. We took Reine for a run round the decks and gave her some bread and milk and put her to bed.

Reine is very excited because it is the first time she has slept in a bunk. She and Josephine have one cabin and I another. Only these beastly selfish expensive English have cabins, the good sound hardy Germans sleep either on deck or in hammocks or in long chairs. It costs them just as much in the end because you see they must buy such quantities of sausages and beer and pies to tide them over the hungers of wakeful nights. But will they be so soppy to have a cabin? They will not. It is quite incorrect for a nordic warrior-soul to lay his padded bones upon the resilience of a mattress however inexpensive (and it is inexpensive). It is incorrect and out of tune with Wotan, hard living and high thought.

As the days go on, long hours split only by meals, sleep-o and the routine of taking Reine for a run round the decks, we, Josephine and I, in a rather desperate boredom that is coming upon us, get to playing two-handed bridge. The weather is not so good. We play and play, sitting in the smoky saloon and some of the time we are beginning to get a little bit. Well, isn't it? We do not exactly quarrel but there is creeping into our conversation an east-wind Gefühl that is not so pleasant. But I will not quarrel. In this way I am perhaps a little tedious for Josephine. I will not quarrel. But the burden of too many stormish interludes is upon me, and the embarrassment of tempers lost and recovered too late. I detest girls who suffer from nerves, I detest stormish interludes. And I have both detestations upon my conscience. But looking at chère Josephine, giving her this sage look out of my weather eye, that has in it, I am suddenly aware, something of kinship to the weather eye of our parrot Joey, that died but recently of angina pectoris, straining upright upon his tail feathers to cry aloud in pain and bewilderment What is come upon me? until we must get the vet to him for an end to his misery, with this weather Joey-eye of mine I behold that Josephine is set for trouble.

I am so fond of Josephine, I so much admire her integrity, in this way that she is never in any least way not Josephine, and I have been friends with her for so long now that I am sure indeed it is not at all the act of a friend to deny her any longer the pleasures of the trouble that she is set for. I am not at all sure for instance that this elegant late husband of Josephine's, dear Jamie, was not in his fear of the blazing blue wrath in Josephine's eyes too little generous in this matter. Too evasive of the trouble that was blowing up from the east side of Josephine's decisive personality.

So I will make haste to shake myself up out of the grave-gravy of my own sadness, and give my little petty-pie all of the trouble for which she is asking. But oh gravy of my *misère*, how leave the enshrouded silences of your *asile* where unlike Titurel I rejoice not, and like him again exist but in suspension?

Well to begin with shall I for a change listen to what Josephine is telling me? Now in journalism was chère Josephine for many years chez this noble Sir Baronet with me and the rest of us. Only she was an editor and not a grand elusive private secretary like me, this editor that was Josephine and Josephine-plus. For need I say, dear Reader, that what with the job-job-job of running a magazine, a husband, a fashionable flat, a maid with the vapours, and the hundred-and-one so-useful social contacts of her then existence, this little angel became somewhat agacée, éreintée, upstage, and off the handle? I guess I need not.

At that time, and how it comes back to me now, our office was for Josephine staffed exclusively by Borgias, Machiavellis, Messalinas, and all the bad boys and girls of history and costume fiction. And *what shall I say to thee, Lord Scroop, thou cruel ingrateful savage and inhuman creature . . . that almost mightst have coined me into gold*, was all her song. And if it wasn't that it was Hamlet, happiest hunting ground for the wrathful righteous whose lot is cast among fools and knaves. *I took thee for thy better. Lecherous treacherous villain, Get thee to a nunnery*. No, no, it is now at once apparent to me, looking back on these past days, and listening again to their recital from the present lips of my overwrought companion, that Josephine's situation was at that time, in the hap of friends enemies and acquaintances, no livelier than the Dane's.

And to her I played Horatio. But even Horatios will turn, and I maintain that this is all so-o-o true, however we are saved the turning point by the death of the hero. And this Horatio-Pompey is going to turn right now, listening for the hundredth-and-how-many-times to the affair of the two ex-editors, bitter unfriends of my Josephine.

These ladies, pleasant and let me hasten to say entirely fictitious characters (so far as this record is concerned), shared a flat in Lanchester Square, W. For all I know they were upright and godfearing, with nothing more on their conscience than frequent log-rolling in the matter of buying and selling each other articles at non-staff rates under assumed names, and taking in each other's family's aspiring sprig's literary advertising and photographic output. Their respective magazines, in a word, were run on this fine old crusted family tradition bent on keeping two homes comfortably together and no offence at all. Indeed no. For if a brother can sell cars, what more like than he should come to giving advice on their upkeep at so much a line, paid for on acceptance;

and if a brother and a sister can between them cover the photogenic lovelies of our upper classes, what more like than they should give first offers at exclusive rates to sister and friend-of-sister editors? *Tritum est* in Fleet Street, and no offence, no offence at all. But when it comes to imputing gross misconduct in private relationships, up go Pompey's hands in trouble-giving dissent and horror, that is what Josephine is so much looking forward to, with so much love of combat and anticipation of conquest or death with honour.

'They lived together, they never went anywhere without each other, they lived in each other's pockets, it is certainly to me extremely unusual to say the least of it that these two . . . Never for a moment out of each other's sight . . . although X absolutely doted on Y and Y . . . And Y . . .'

Well according to Josephine Y got a poor deal, doing all the hard work with the lovey-dovey insistence of the too-devoted. Josephine draws to her climax:

'Of course I am not saying Pompey for one moment that there were actually any *vicious practices*.'

Hurra. Hurra three times. Now it is all out.

'No vicious practices, no my grandmother. Josephine you are off your head.'

The veil of imaginative fiction thus rent unfriendlywise in twain, Josephine is almost at the point of tears.

'Pompey.'

'Josephine.'

But these two harmless ladies, kind to each other, united in the care of unresponsive cats, united in love of families and the promotion of their at least material wellbeing, to impute to them, so well known to me, and at the moment retired in modest affluence to Eastbourne, this quelquechose de Lesbos is so very laughable, I can no longer offer to Josephine any drawn sword of hostility for offence or defence. I rush out of the cabin and tear up to the bridge deck, there leaning out far astern I watch the seagulls come flapping flapping eagerly in the ship's wake for the breadcrumbs I left below. Oh darling seagulls, wide-winged disagreeable and voracious, I am so sorry, so very sorry about these breadcrumbs, but go down for them again I will not, so to-night you must go supperless to bed, rocking with empty bellies on the waves of the Baltic, and thinking no doubt Josephine's dark thoughts of Pompey the deceiver.

But go down to the cabin, go down to the cabin again I must, to speak again to Josephine who is sitting all forlorn upon the edge of the bunk, crying quietly into a Fortnum and Mason chiffon handkerchief. Oh Josephine I am so very sorry that I am so boring for you now, and how many times have I not told you the same banal stories, the same so-delicious shop-talk that is to be repeated over and over again and never to be thought of for one moment to be interrupted in this barbarous manner by this stuff and nonsense hullaballoo. Why it is a ladies' and gentlemen's agreement, sink me if I need say more. Why, do not Harriet and I for instance nightly regale ourselves with the same so-o-o boring personalities that are not in the moment of telling boring at all, but a sweet delight and a stalwart bulwark against the tread of time? And does it do harm to the harmless dotty ladies and gentlemen who are all our song? Indeed it does not. Better to be preserved in infamous memory however fictitious than buried in the grave-gravy of sadness and oblivion.

Darling Pompey, must we have this grave-gravy joke again? Did we not perhaps have it for once too often several pages back, and is it in essence so extremely funny-ha-ha that it will bear this so-frequent repetition?

But it is something so exquisite so simple and so *bonhomme* you must suffer your Pompey to have this light to layten the derkness of her grave of sadness.

I am now concerned with Josephine because I have made her cry. I have done something at which the crocodile . . .

I have broken the gentlemen's agreement of all

the shops, and especially of the Fleet Street shop that is so concerned with personalities, I have cried Stuff and Nonsense in the sacred places. I am an abomination and a desolation in the clear stream of slander, and what should I expect when next myself I presume upon the unwritten privilege of a free hearing and no offence, no offence in the world. Oh Josephine I am so sorry. So we go to the saloon and have a drink. And Josephine is so kind and so large-minded that our friendship settles at once upon an easy keel. Affectionate practical intelligent Josephine, how much I count on you, my pet, if you only knew it, but how tell you without blowing the gaff on my own chaotic thoughts?

We make a night of it in the saloon, we drink to Tilssen to the future to my health and hers, secretly I tip the glass to sanity security escape and return.

We are beyond the Danziger Bucht, we are out of Germany, we have arrived. We must take off in a row-boat because the water is so shallow. It is only creeping gently knee-high over the white sands. There is a little fringe of dark bush above the low cliffs. The village clusters above again, and beyond high on its hilltop sits the Schloss of our good-health. We have arrived in time for tea, and tea we have, of a peculiarly unsatisfying consistency. We sit in the large salon of the Schloss, it is an extremely lofty room and the windows run down to the floor and open upwards upon a terrace. There are people in the room but I will not look at them, soon enough, too soon they must become for me not people but individuals, differentiated, separate, friends and unfriends. They can wait. Josephine takes Reine. We go to our rooms. Oh this weariness of arriving, and weariness and aggravation of new scenes and fresh faces thronging upon thought. My room is secure and private. I lock the door. It is as quiet as the grave, as secure as silent. The grave's a fine and private place. But none, I think, do there embrace. O.K. I should not wish it otherwise. I take off my hat and coat and frock. Bathe my face in eau-de-cologne, lie down upon the bed and at once I am asleep and dreaming.

I dream, it is about Freddy. It is like this. I am sitting at night-time in a dark room, it is lighted by one candle that is stuck in a bottle on a trestle table, I am sitting at the table, I am turning over papers, so many papers, there are hundreds of papers, but it is frightful it is something absolutely frightful how many of these papers there are. They are forms to be filled in, questions to be answered, there is so much detail and all the time I am feeling, am knowing for certain, that there is so little time and still so much to be done with so much of care and accuracy and no mistake to be made that will not involve penalty of conscience and a general calamity. But how many forms, how many questions. I have a shade over my eyes and I am in uniform. But it is a secret, this uniform, it must not for a moment appear that I am in uniform, it is an official secret of some higher command, it is a sealed order, and to me something that is not perfectly assimilated, why I am here, why I am in uniform. So to me comes across the room this dream Freddy, that is looking so sweet and winning, as in his most amiable minute of some months, some many months ago. He stands above me at the table and looks down upon me. Why Pompey, you are in uniform. No, Freddy, my sweet darling Freddy why you are raving, Uniform? Why certainly you are dotty. This is not uniform, why these for instance are my riding clothes. What are the stars on your collar? Why these are not stars, these are the pin heads of the pin that keeps my tie in place. From whom is your commission? Why I hold no commission, why surely you could not be so dippy, to think that I am sitting here under orders from an authority I do not know I do not recognize to exist? I hold no commission. By God I swear it. By the blood of Christ, by the true cross, by the Host upon the altar. I stand up to shout at him, to perjure myself upon all that is nameless. Why come on, my sweet boy, why here is just Pompey in her riding clothes, sitting late into the night, to the sweet tune of the thoughts that come and go, sitting here by the light of the candle, to think and think.

But he shakes his head, he looks so sad, he is so sweet, and already he is fading away from my dream-sight, and the stars on my collar are burning bright, fire-bright white light of fire heat, burning, piercing, tearing, to burn the flesh from the bones, and burn and burn.

And I think of the high princess in the story, with her coronet of flame fast bound to hair and head, and the long robe swinging, and the flames licking and swinging, and turning upon the flesh.

But in my dream-reality my star flame does not burn my flesh, it burns and flares and scorches upon my mind in its bewilderment of weariness, and the insistence of the questions that must be answered upon the forms upon the table.

But as I turn again to these my dream fades and I sink again into a deeper sleep, where if the dreams must come, let them come, they are at a deeper level, to be forgotten upon waking in a general incoherence and not to be recalled.

One night after we had been at Tilssen for several weeks I had this dream again, identical, in every detail the same. It was early in the morning when I woke, and still dark. I do not dream very often, and rarely so clearly. I sat up in bed and switched the light on. And sitting up in my bed in that hard unsentimental light of the unshaded bulb, I thought about Freddy and the pains and backsweep of remorse that is always being so much a part of unhappy love. The war-motive in this dream did not at all trouble me or weigh in upon my consciousness.

'Are we a good soldier?' said my doctor to me one day, about to make an injection in my left arm.

Pompey very very bad soldier. There I knew it, and never had it occurred to me in reason that I should at any time be a soldier either good or bad.

But this return of Freddy, with a ghostlike reality above and transcending the usual dream image, this was very profoundly disturbing. I thought that I had left him behind in England, with the rights and the wrongs of it as between the two of us unsolved but shelved. Into that again I will not go, never, never never, farewell again everlasting farewells to that unhappy image.

But at once, deceitful mind, up springs the living memory of the last time we were together. I have a more actual memory for scenery than for faces, for the feel of the earth than for the feel of a human being, and this last vivid memory brings to my nose the scent of grass and to my touch the harshness of the ground on which I lay, on which I lay, as I am lying now upon my bed in Tilssen, but not then alone. That memory is too painful, but yet I am so wide awake and how keep thought at bay? I get up and go to the window and pull back the curtains to look out across the sea. Very desolate and cold is the night view upon the moonlit tumbled waters, for there is a high wind blowing and the white capped waves are far out across the bay. But though I am so much and so solidly you would say upon the floor of my bedroom in this distant country, my feet prick to the feel of Hertfordshire earth baked into square cakes by the summer sunshine, and the earth takes the weight of my feet, and my toes are pricked by the stiff grass that thrusts up through my sandals.

Both feet in Hertfordshire – and what then has Tilssen and what sort of monstrum horrendum informe ingens cui lumen ademptum is this Pompey that is so sick to death of this bright bright light that is burning down upon her from the naked bulb? I turn restlessly intolerably from the window. I am sick of this room and the bright light and the way I am so wide awake and do not want to lie down upon the bed.

I decide that I will go downstairs, I will take a night walk, and if I meet anyone it shall appear to be for the usual reason of night walks. And what is that? dear Reader, you are too polite to ask. I guess it is just a bad fourth form joke, or the joke that they have in the hotels: Gentlemen are requested to be in their own rooms by 6 o'clock pour ne pas scandaliser les femmes de chambre, those sensitive plants of exigeant morals.

Dressing-gown and slippers. Here is Pompey on the ramp and already feeling better because she has actually made up her mind, a something that she has not done for some time past, to the confusion not only of her own mind but of her so-dear friends and relations. Well here I am on the ramp. The light is out, the door is closed behind me, I have a pocket torch, thoughtful good-bye present from the Lion of Hull. I blow her a kiss of thankyou to far away Bottle Green.

Down the enormous stone staircase I go, pad, pad. But the modern conveniences, so spick and span, so uproarious in action, are not upon the ground floor, well for that matter neither are the bedrooms, so I am afraid we shall have to throw overboard Jokes One and Two. I cross the enormous hall – yes, everything in this Schloss is in scale gargantuan – I go through the door, again across a long corridor and down some more stairs, my nocturnal marauding is leading me, I should suspect, to the pantry. I shall most certainly raid it, for I am getting yes I am getting a little bit hungry. And that springs to my mind at once not as a joke but as a fact and more than a fact an excuse, if necessary.

I am as nervous as a cat, as a young cat that is about to be sucked up the chimney by a puff of draught from under the door. I turn the handle, open the door and flash my torch straight into the eyes of Tom Satterthwaite.

Tom Satterthwaite, Major Satterthwaite to the old ladies, is one of the few people who have separated themselves from the massed faces of our fellow guests and invalids. Josephine and I rather like him, indeed I thought at one time that Josephine . . . but it was only a little thought, why it was just a little thought that hardly had its eyes open, that was so small.

Josephine and I have made friends with Haidée von Borck, the chic little Baronin from Berlin, and we have all been sailing and swimming together and enjoying the long summer days, and more than the long summer days, and infinitely longer, the endless combinations and permutations of the possible and impossible characteristics of this mysterious Tom-Tom. For he is in a small way a mystery that would never impinge upon our consciousness if we had not these so-long days and evenings with little to do and the sickly sweet smell of invalidismus in our nostrils.

No, I do not mean that the Schloss stinks of iodoform and cabbage water, it certainly does not, but there is always the so-to-say spiritual aroma of sickness that as we get stronger and fatter in the salt sea air comes a thought unpleasant to the three of us.

But there does not appear to be anything at all the matter with dear Tom. He is hale and hearty and as fat as butter, not too fat, but fat enough to please at least Josephine and me, who have too much of the skeleton in ourselves not to appreciate its concealment in others. The clatter of jowl on jowl has little aesthetic pleasure outside of the midnight fancies of Edgar Allan Poe.

But if he is so hale and hearty, what is he doing here, and he will go off for long days at a time, and alone, or at least we think he is alone, or is it that we are already this much involved, that we like to think him alone? But what is he doing here and what is he doing here at this unchristian hour?

With his fair poll, his air of exuberant ben essere, his engaging plumpness, his candid eyes, darling Tom I can already hardly remember this first meeting, so much, so very much has happened since. But it must have been exciting, I think, even then for the first time to sit and talk and eat the bread and cheese we have found in the pantry. But why do you sit in the light of a candle at this little table, writing, writing, my sweet Tom? That thought must certainly have crossed my mind if not my lips, but then he says, I remember how at once it is something we have in common, how much he hates the hard light that shines down from the electric light bulbs.

And there is something curious that in this famous Kurhaus the light is always being so particularly hard and brilliant, so death and destruction to happy thought and the sweet doze that waits upon it. So hard, so hard are these lights that at evening in the drawing-room we sit like puppets, the old ladies with their tatting, their *petit point*, their patience, and Haidée and Josephine and I with our books, until we must go out we can bear it no longer, for the hard light that is so exacting and so ferocious in its constant down-beating brilliance sucks the life out of us, leaving us without power of thought or action, dead and yet alive, unable to stir and yet over-sentient to the slight noise of the knitting needles, the frou-frou of a skirt shifting its folds, the dead inanimate noises that are so much alive, and we so dead.

How often at night, by what effort of will saving ourselves alive from the spell that is cast upon us, have we not run out of the room, out of the great wide doors, down the steps and across the cliffs and beach, there to find our sailing boat, our darling *Baranar* 2 (and where is *Baranar* 1? we cannot tell), and raising sail under a high moon we have gone to sail and sail across the waters away from the great room, away from the old ladies, Mrs. Farmer, Mrs. Pouncer, Miss Hatt and Lady Pym. Yes, we have by now separated quite a number of our fellow guests, but these old ladies, they are rather fascinating you know, I am having this *tendre* for the old ladies.

Mrs. Pouncer is my especial favourite. She is a very pretty old lady, with a great care for her dress and appearance, she dresses mostly in plum colours, in puce, magenta, mulberry and vieux rose, she has very small hands and feet and little ears that come out of her peruke de style, that bear, white and delicate as they are, a weight of ancestral ruby upon ancestral setting. But Pouncer – fascinating name, she must have a little black dog-doggie, I think he is called Mamilian, yes, I think he must have this grand traditional name, yes, perhaps she is a witch.

But when at night I am sailing with Haidée and Josephine across the sea and far away on the wings of our *Baranar* 2, up so far and far away that we must surely very soon come to Lapland, we forget the cold hard spell in the lofty drawing room, and the figures frozen in the cold hard light, and the figures that move their hands a little, and their feet a little, and sigh a little and cough, but all in this peculiar little way as if one should say: How clever the automatons are, the slight movement is quite lifelike, very extraordinary and clever is it not? And I wonder what *They* will think of next?

When I am in that room I too wonder what *They* will think of next, and I am not anticipating at all that it will be a very pleasant thought that is to come next, to-day or to-morrow perhaps or a month ahead.

But now all *our* thought is the sea and the spume and the racing boat, that has very exact and narrow lines, and can mount and run through the water so swiftly and so delicately that there is very little of a wake behind us, and we move so swiftly, so deliciously, it is a very highest pleasure to us.

But Haidée von Borck is an excellent sailor and under her tutelage Josephine and I are also becoming, if not so clever so dashing so precise, at least no longer a mere huddle of passenger-flesh. There is too just a little danger, you know, in this wild sailing on a windy night that is a little bit pleasant and sends a current of swift blood through our veins, so this serves at last entirely to dispel the horrible feeling of the castle drawing-room where we had hardly veins at all or blood to run in them.

Now there is, also separated and made into an individual at this grand Schloss, a Colonel Peck that is always being so extremely absent minded, it is a neurosis with him, the poor man, it is sad for him to be this way so very much unaware of the daily life. He is for instance entirely dependent upon his spectacles, for without them he can see nothing very clearly, so that without them the physical world must indeed present to him the reflection of his permanently distracted mind. But always he is searching for these spectacles, it is like Psyche who looked the world over for her lover, and he comes into the room where we are sitting and he says . . . No, first he stands awhile in the door letting the abominable draught from the open hall and wide staircase to come blowing in upon us, and he says, standing there and peering myopic eye upon what unfocussed vision we cannot guess (And even if these spectacles were here, even if they were for instance in front of him upon the writing table, could he see them?) So he says: Not here I fear.

You see, just that: *Not here I fear*. And does this give the last turn to our screw that is driving in upon us on these unbearable long evenings chez Schloss, does this give to us the last and utterly last feeling of unsubstantiality that must put us deeper into our frozen fastnesses or on happier occasions send us flying for sanity and movement to the open sea? Yes it does and it does.

Well no doubt on the first night I met Tom to talk to him in the kitchen cellarage we talked of this and of this fear of the naked light and of this Colonel Peck and these old ladies, and of Josephine and Haidée, and swooping back on a long homeward flight, of London and of the many people there that he knows and that I know, of Herman and Rosa Blum, my musical friends of many parties, of Gustav, of Larry the Pansy, of Henry.

After this night I often rode out with Tom in the early mornings, to come back to Haidée and Josephine for breakfast coffee and rolls in the little glasshouse annexe to the dining room, where sitting all together as happy and friendly as you please we lay plans for other happy days of picnics and boating and swimming and excursions to the little university town of Ool where the students have been getting rather excited lately, and excited and showing off, with large banners and demonstrations and high gestures and much talk.

But these rides with Tom are a very great happiness for me and already I have not for a long time had one soppy thought of strain and turmoil and Oh Life, Life, and monster of my dreams, and Oh horror of fear and of thought coming upon thought from some far place that is not, is not heaven.

Long happy hours of summertime, oh darling Tilssen of those long August days, empty of all significance but the minute upon the minute, how happy I was then, how spendthrift of these happy minutes, with no thought but for that present time, freed for once of the tyranny of ideas, indeed it was to be born again into the careless heritage of the once born, with no otherway thought to come with wracking twisting and tormenting malice. For Josephine, Haidée, Reine and me, it was to be completely free, in a firm light friendship, not emotionally held at all, but carelessly, lightly, in the friendship of a happy schoolday. All summer in a schoolday that has this to point the moral, that you are let out from school on a whole day's exeat to keep the head mistress's birthday, it may be, or the death of a governing bishop. And so with a sorrowful or a happy face, made up to suit the occasion, you run away to take out the boat, to swim, ride or picnic, and the face that left the school chapel with all of the official occasion writ up upon it, soon can tell another story, of happiness in freedom, of unconscious happiness.

But no Pompey of this world can long be so quiet and docile but must turn round upon herself and her darling little friends to make trouble and disturbance. So now for me my morning rides with Tom became of increasing importance. And if with Josephine and Haidée the years fell away from me and I re-experienced something of a happy childhood, with Tom it was quite entirely different altogether. I watched him closely and he watched me closely, on these morning rides we were a little wary of each other. To begin with I was quite infatuated with his really splendid appearance, I could not tell if he was very intelligent or not, nor did I care, being by this time a little shy of intelligence and prepared to jettison all such dotty ideas in the full appreciation of this beautiful Tom boy. His conversation was not, dear Reader, the sort of thing that clever people like us can cope with for long. But might it not be a *concealing* stupidity, deliberately adopted for some purpose? It lacked the engaging candour of bone-stupidity, but as I had at that time no key to his motive for adopting any thought-mask of any sort, I let it go, I let it go and became so completely and childishly infatuated by this grand form and feature of Tom-Tom that I cared very little what was in his mind.

This morning we rode up to the fort again. He is very devoted to this ride. We go up the hill past the church and up and up, and striking off through the pine woods we come after two hours' riding to this aged fort that has the guns still set in it, rusty and of a very ancient vintage, I should suppose, and bearing the encouraging name of a well known English firm. It is this very hot hot August day and so we get off and have something out of Tom's flask, and we have our picnic lunch too, for it is 12 o'clock now and after two hours in the saddle we are hot and tired. Afterwards we climb up on to the roof of the fortress, wriggling and squirming with very little of foothold and so we come out on to the roof.

'You can command the whole valley from here, taking in the little town of Ool as well as Tilssen,' says dear Tom.

I turn my wary Joey-eye upon him.

He is thinking of gun emplacements, and now I think suddenly that beneath his happy rather inane talky-talk that has been going on for so many of these hours we have spent together, there is always this something else in his mind that has perhaps always something to do with gun emplacements and this sort of thing that is rather Greek to me, and rather sad too in its unpleasant associations and the way it is so often driving a wedge between the sort of work that is men's work and the sort of work that is women's work, and all of that line of reasoning that is so a part of unhappy fighting times and of cheap newspaper correspondence columns. Phew, how I do detest this. Never again in England I think shall we breed exclusively masculine and exclusively feminine types at any high level of intelligence, but always there will be much of the one in the other and often it is making me laugh to see how not only the men sometimes in a very tired moment of irritation but often the women too are saying Oh how much they long for the time to come again when there was nothing of this subtle overlapping at all but everything was as plain as a pikestaff, and there was no little pet Larry to sing his Green Sleeves, his Polish Ma, his Tirry Lirry down the Lane and to whisper with what of maiden *Schwärmerei* the passion he is entertaining for his high-up naval officer. Oh Larry is the boy to put the kettle on and when the tea comes freshly made in little pot on little tray to tell the tale of love at full tide happy in surmise. For here in him is the true touch of the feminine, how much happier is this momentous affair in the minute of surmise than it can ever come to be in actuality. But my women friends when they indulge themselves in this nostalgie for the past that was perhaps not so aktuell as they imagine are not at great pains to conceal the cause of their disturbance and always God in Heaven before very long it will come out, how it is that they have lost heavily on the Stock Exchange or it is an editor and she has had her pet contributor stolen away from her, or the circulation of her paper has dropped, and so it is the song of: Oh for anything but this. And with the men who are not Larrys it is the same, they have suffered trials and losses, in their emotions perhaps, but more likely in their finances, and so it is the song of: Oh for anything but this.

But my women friends are very cunning, oh very astute are these little pets, that so well contrive to make the best of both worlds, concealing a masculine intention in a feminine phrase, a thought in a word. They are perhaps just a trifle better at this game than the men, oh just a trifle, just a tiny little trifle that hardly has its eyes open.

And at a high level of intelligence it is a game and

can afford to be a game, for intelligence is sexless and has its own weapons, and these are well matched, and if the women are clever in the way I have said to make the best of both worlds, the men see the point well enough and can afford to laugh. They can laugh. It is a game. But at a low level of intelligence, God help us all, there there is a very crudèle extremity of ill-feeling and a wilderness of tears. But it is unfortunate how it is that stupid people are so often having a very remarkable physical vitality and so must continue, and must continue, to be a dirge and a disturbance.

And can they be quiet and skilful to make the best of all possible worlds? They can not. But the more masculine of the women will wear pants and stiff collars and be an offence to the eye, and the more feminine of the men will pretend to be so masculine it would surprise you, and they will prance round and dress up in coloured shirts and talk a lot about Jews and women for a dirge and a disturbance of all peace. And the women in their pants will prance round and they will also talk too, oh yes, they will have a lot to say, oh yes, and mostly it will be a pseudo-feminist talk to put you out of your mind with irritation. For by their clothes they would wish to approximate so closely to the masculine physique – and to whom for a good might that be? And it is really to make you laugh or be sick to see in tight pants the large feminine behind that is so much a contradiction of what at their low level of intelligence these rampageous little fatheads are out to pursue. I hope they will come up with their Chimera and that he will turn and rend them and turn and with his long strong yellow teeth tear them to pieces and bite and bite until there is nothing left of their little feminine bones that have been protesting a great deal too much.

Oh if there is to be anything of pleasure at all in the sweet uses of heterosexuality, please remember to be feminine, darling Miss or Mrs., but once out of bed, pursue your own way, but do not make such a fuss up, it is for a dirge and disturbance of all peace.

Thinking these sad thoughts of the flag-wavers of both sexes I came running down the staircase at Schloss Tilssen to have tea with Josephine, my darling civilized tib cat of a Josephine, with Haidée and with Reine.

As I round the corner to come in through the doorway into the lounge there is the telephone in its kiosk and in the kiosk telephoning is Colonel Peck, but he is speaking, but his voice comes through the glass doors, I can hear him, I can hear what he is saying, but he is speaking German, but this does not at first convey very much to me as I stand to listen. I stand to listen because his voice, this Colonel Peck voice, is suddenly become so incisive, so very un-absentminded, so very unlike the vagueness of Colonel Peck, that I am amazed and so in my great surprise at this uncharacteristic voice that is so completely foreign to the picture we have built up on the very most circumstantial of evidence the picture of this distracted Colonel Peck, I must stand and listen. For suddenly a thought comes into my mind that is tying itself up with other thoughts that have not quite become thoughts, not in a complete consciousness. And what is he saying, what is he saying in this quick incisive voice in German? He is saying: Er sagte dasz er es tun wolle, wenn er könne. Also bitte den Brief wieder zu mir zusenden Es ist zu ihm addressiert. Nicht? Also, bitte. Ja, ja, ich weiss dass er abgereist ist. There is a long pause, he says nothing, then: Also, bis Sonntag. And down goes the handset with a profoundly un-absentminded clatter, and out of his box comes the Colonel. I am by this time across the lounge you can guess, I am sitting down to look at the *Bystander*. Colonel Peck has seen me and is become at once again this absentminded Colonel Peck that is now so familiar. Hallo, Miss Casmilus, having tea in here to-day?

No, I say, I am just waiting for Baronin von Borck. Oh, she's out on the verandah with your friend, Mrs. . . . (this is Josephine), at least I am nearly sure I saw them together, and the little girl, when I came through just now. I invite him to have tea with us because he is a pleasant old man, or at least the familiar up-to-now-absentminded Colonel Peck has made that impression upon us all, so that I know Josephine and Haidée will like to have him to tea. So out we go.

Josephine makes a great fuss of him to have his tea exactly as he likes it, and talks and makes up to him a little, for Josephine has this faible for old colonels just as I have my faible for old ladies, if they are pretty and not too exasperatingly loquacious.

So the talk drifts round and about, and there is this and that to be said, and we all have our parts to play, but every now and then Colonel Peck glances at me, and he is not wearing his spectacles, that have no doubt once again eluded this poor Psyche that cannot find his true love, but for all that and all that the spectacles are not upon his nose, the glance he gives me is keen enough, and I think he misses very little, and I think he is wondering a little about that so-incisive telephoning, and wondering perhaps if I was all the time so wrapt up in my *Bystander* as not to hear and not myself to wonder. So there is here a little cross-current of thought. But presently the talk drifts to the situation as it is now so full of danger, and the threat of war as it is now in the Mediterranean. And first Josephine was talking about Mussolini and how much better the trains are running in Italy now, for when she was last over there I get the impression they never ran at all, but only strolled about looking to find a nice place for a lie-down and a good sleep. And then she is getting rather cross about Abyssinia. And so here I must point out to her, but just to be so annoying for poor Josephine I must say: But do not be so cross with Mussolini because certainly it is through him and through this African adventure of his that has for him had a successful outcome, it is through this that we without one stroke of war now have Egypt again within our hands in such a way as she has not been in our hands since the war, and no offence no offence to anyone at all, that this grand piece of arrangement has made us again the master of Egypt and thrown into our hands all that convenient coast-line as well as the vast hinterland that runs up again, it is so convenient, to the ultimate last outpost of lower Egypt, with the Nile for our river and the whole vast darkness of middle Africa to link up maybe with our East African dependencies – oh so charming is this word dependency, how fascinating I find it. And by and by running ever southwards and downwards you will come to the Cape which was another oh so good arrangement though we are only so sorry that here we blundered a little to have something so crude as a war, and a war as the grand Prince Von has said not so entirely as usual on the right side of the world's conscience till there came C. B. to put that right. And now for the Mediterranean there are these further grand arrangements that are to be made to make also the north bank of it dependable if not dependant, and for this reason came running the Turkish Minister running to London to a secret conference. So that will be all right too and no offence, no offence. And war? My dear chap don't be hysterical. War? We've got past all that, we are not so crude nowadays, we are not so crude at all. But there has been this Turkish arrangement and this Egyptian arrangement and if Mussolini in his Roman fury but little of Roman policy has accomplished this for us, and for himself but a patch of infertile and unquiet territory, have we so much to be so annoyed about? Why, I think we should be very grateful to him, yes I think we should say Tnahkyou Mussolini. For also for our close neighbour he has given us a secure government and now perhaps the Kenya settlers will not so much grumble that their labour gangs are slave-raided and slave-raided again and again from across the Abyssinian frontier. But sleep lion, sleep thou British animal, for all is quiet all is secure and your servants have served you very well, dream not of Mediterranean disturbance at the harsh word of Josephine and Colonel Peck. You have every reason to sleep in a deep sleep of peace, security and consolidated interests.

Colonel Peck is listening with a quiet smile. He might be the British Lion himself he looks so sleek. He is smiling.

And on whose side are you?

I am on the side of my friends, for if they win they are the people I should choose to live with. And who fights to lose? And often a principle may seem wrong, a national policy is antipathetic to the sensitive conscience of the individual. But it is the sensitive conscience that must abrogate, and in time of war I fight with my friends, with the people I like, with the people I can live with. How dreadful in the pursuit of a presumptuous principle to find that you have fought and won and the victory is yours, but look it is a victory for your principle, and the people your fellow fighters how very much you may hate them, oh but it is possible indeed always it has happened in my experience it has happened. In principle I believed in Irish freedom but oh how I detest the hysteria and the malice and the *Schwärmerei* of that movement. And oh how I detested then, so that I must withdraw from the movement, my fellow enthusiasts, who would I make no bones have died upon a hundred barricades, but not I with them.

'And the Jews?' says Colonel Peck, and Tom Satterthwaite has come up too, he is sitting at the table with us, and Josephine has poured him out a lovely cup of tea that she has ordered to be fresh made for him.

Ah the Jews, the Jews. No I will not be drawn.

'Come on Pompey,' says Tom. 'And the Jews?'

I am in despair for the racial hatred that is running in me in a sudden swift current, in a swift tide of hatred, and Out out damned tooth, damned aching tooth, rotten to the root.

Do we not always hate the persecuted?

Would any but they have survived their persecutions? Oh devilish hateful jibe, oh how it tugs at my assent. 'None but the Jews would have survived their persecutions.' Immense differentiation of the would and could. The would points to pride and death in honourable suicide, the Would of history and Colonel Peck is tugging at my heart and brain.

But I have had some very dear Jewish friends.

Oh final treachery of the smug goy. Do not all our persecutions of Israel follow upon this smiling sentence?

'And yet and yet you would not I think,' says Tom, 'no I do not think that you would throw in your lot with them to fight with them, however in theory and mercy justifiable their cause?'

The virtue has gone out of me. Dully stupidly I bend my head. They are true these words, they are right these two soldiers with whom indeed I have little very little in common, they are quite and absolutely right. Stupidly, reiteratively, I say:

'I will fight with my friends my true friends my

real friends the people with whom I am happy.'

'And these are not Jews?'

'No.'

'It is a sort of loyalty in you, Pompey,' says Tom, 'that seeing the drift of policies, and the argument of history, you will still fight with your friends.'

No it is not loyalty, not so much loyalty as this, it is a half perceived truth, that friendship is a more final truth than policy or the argument of history, for it goes deeper than either and touches to the root of something that we cannot completely understand or completely assess or explain, and compared with which policy is the most frivolous of tea-cup chatter.

How cold are the delights of the moon. This evening the electric wires have fused and all of those hard cruel electric lights that have made night life at the Schloss so much a trial and an exacerbation are now powerless to injure. We sit in the enormous drawing-room, the old ladies cannot do their embroidery, Josephine, Haidée and I cannot read our books, we cannot make up a four to play bridge with Colonel Peck, so in more comfort and quietness and quiet companionship than ever before we sit in the great drawing-room gathered in a wide open semi-circle round the wide hearth, for it is September now and the nights grow cold and in the hearth there is burning an enormous wood fire, the logs sizzle and there is the soft fluff-fluff of burning wood turning upon ash and falling falling through the iron grating.

It is very quiet and pleasant. There upon the right of me is the window, and the high full moon riding up out of the sea shines through the slats of the long venetian blinds. But I am a little unquiet again in my head, I am really a little sad for something that is not quite yet come upon me to be fully realized, I am very unquiet. And presently I get up and run out of the room alone, and alone I run down to the cliffs, and sitting there at the base of the pine trees I am feeling very sad and unruhig indeed, and I am beginning to cry again. Yes here it is again, as if I had never been better, never healed again of the sadness I had in England, before I came running off in this foolish adventure with chère Josephine.

And I think of our talk at tea time and to what am I committed, oh what did I say then and what was it that came up in my so savage heart? And I twist my hands and cry, I cannot stop, indeed it is a flood that brings no peace no peace and no surcease from pain at all.

A stupid line from an ineffable stupid poem that

was on some ballad sheet I had some long time ago comes into my head further to infuriate me in my savage mood. 'When tear-washed hearts recapture bliss.' Oh yes? That is a good idea? Yes? Oh yes. And if they do not recapture bliss – eh? That is not so good. Listen now this is what I say, remembering the chapter in Ecclesiastes which suddenly I now am come to understand:

In a shower of tears I sped my fears
And lost my heavy pain
But now my grief that knew relief
Is sultried o'er again.

Of fruit and flower of that first shower
No memories remain
The clouds hang down in heavy frown
But still it does not rain.

Happy the man of simple span
Whose cry waits on his pain
But there are some whose mouths are dumb
When the clouds return again.

How is that? Is not that better in expression but in truth how sad?

How cold are the delights of the moon, already the tears are frozen upon my cheeks. I think of the prayer to Artemis that is gallant and conventional in the Greek manner but has nothing in it of the heart, And of pain for the stain of the evil twined round the heart, the heart that was slain. And I try to say a Christian prayer but I am come very far from that and it falls athwart my memory stumbling slantwise into consciousness. Almighty God that art ever more willing to hear than we to pray and dost forgive the souls of them that depart hence in the Lord, create and make in us new and contrite hearts that we surely trusting in thy defence may not fear the power of any evil but study to preserve thy people committed to his charge in wealth peace and godliness.

The words come tumbling aslant and the trees' leaves move in the wind, there is a feeling of laughter in the fall of the trees' leaves upon the wind. And no wonder no wonder at all, for what I have said is very ridiculously wrong, very funny-ha-ha indeed, that would make a pine tree laugh. Oh is it not funny the way this prayer has got itself mixed in with two prayers to make life very bright and funny and not vulgar at all, for the pine trees it is just a wholesome joke. So I begin to laugh now. But really it is quite ridiculous.

Very witty this painter, is he not?

What did you say, what did you say there Pompey? Why now, remember to be very careful here, oh please to remember to be so careful, because this Painter Business circles in the widest outsweeping strong flight to the very first words that you have written. But on what a trajectory, to attain such an encirclement, to hit back to the beginning, oh what an enormous great parabola you have described. And on the way, what was there on the way, that has turned your lips so pale, where were you then, where was the colour struck from those two lips, that are not yet much withered?

I am back again within the picture-gallery, to look and see and wish so much to have the amusing canvases they have hung there.

Very witty this painter, is he not?

Very witty this Georg Grosz, very funny-ha-ha indeed.

And the old men that are not hung in that gallery, the old men that are hung high upon their crutches for an after-war memorial and a Post War Museum, only within my memory to live again and never be forgotten? Are they not also very funny-ha-ha, very bracing and astringent indeed, to come to us, to tell us, Es war einmal ein Krieg, Es war einmal ein Krieg we never knew?

Oh war war is all my thought. And suddenly I am very alert and not dreaming now asleep at all, but very awake and for ever more, and not dreaming again at all, to wring my hands and cry, but very practical I am become. Achtung, achtung! I hope that I am very practical.

For suddenly my sleeping dreaming eyes are open very wide, and my thoughts that left me on a wide high upreaching flight, to shoot so high and curve downwards on a long trajectory to the beginning of my thought, have come home to me to wait, very tensed, very alert and practical. Leave me no more, oh truant thoughts, cross-trailing to eternity through the wide cold corridors of outer space, but come home to me now, to stay within my head, very cold, very reasonable indeed, tensed and very practical.

Pompey, Pompey.

It is this clever and pursuing Tom who is calling to me as I sit here in the white strange cold moonlight of the full moon over the sea, I can hear his voice and I can hear his feet crashing through the undergrowth.

'Here, Tom,' I cry, calling his name with a drawling pause to make almost two syllables out of that uncompromising Tom. 'To-om, To-om.' He breaks through the circle of trees and comes and sits beside me. He flashes his torch into my eyes close up to my face, my pupils dilate in the bright hard torchlight. It is not so necessary, indeed it is not, for the moonlight is so bright, so bright, like daylight but cold, cold.

He puts the torch back in his pocket and takes my two hands that are so cold, and the tears are still frozen on my cheeks. It is so cold on this late

September night for we are far to the north and already winter is upon the air riding down upon us from the white north, so cold, so very cold and strange.

Tom is talking, quietly, with great empressement, very quietly and quickly, very constrainingly, he holds my hands in a tight grip, I cannot pull away, I cannot look away, the white moonlight shines down upon us both.

'Why Pompey, my dear girl, my dear Pompey, so now you are wide awake and now you will listen, won't you, and not go drifting away, fading away, so quietly so quickly so effectively evasive, no that you will not do. Now listen, Pompey, do you hear it?'

I do not have to listen, oh yes, I hear it very well, I am thinking now that I have always heard it, oh yes I hear it very well.

'Tell me, Pompey.'

It is 40 miles away, and moving northwards, they are firing at close intervals, then there is a break, then they begin again, it is a little uneven, they are not perhaps very good, not so good as they should be, but perhaps the guns are old, yes perhaps they are as old as the guns up at the fort, and perhaps again they have not the same good name upon them.

'What name, Pompey?'

'Birdie, Birdie, Strand and Dolland.'

Tom is laughing; 'So you noticed that, yes you

actually came awake to notice that did you? There never was such a girl for noticing and not noticing. And all those long hours we rode out together, up past the church, through the pine woods, past the dam up and up to the fort and the old guns, you remember that, yes? And the long careful lectures I gave you, all that valuable military talky-talk for beginners, interspersed with hoary wisecracks to draw your pity if not your attention, your long side glances, your Poor Tom, poor Tom, wary-Joey-eye look? You remember that too, eh?'

'Wary-Joey-eye?' I say. 'Why surely Tom you did not know about our Joey parrot that died, that stood upright upon his tail feathers, to stand upright and cry aloud: "What is come upon me?" '

Swiftly swiftly Tom's grip on my two hands tightens, quickly he speaks.

'Now Pompey for heaven's sake don't go thinking about poor Joe that died and is at peace in the seventh of Joey-heavens. Yes, you told me about him, yes certainly you did. But listen, listen.'

My thoughts are trailing off again, swiftly to rise and get away, to get away on the wings of deceased Joey-bird, away from the compelling the so-constraining urgent voice of Tom. But they are tethered, they cannot fly, my thoughts cannot rise up to be off to no good purpose, they are tethered to the two hands that hold my hands in strength and urgency to compel to compel and force my thoughts upon his thought.

He is speaking now for a long time and I understand I understand very well what he is saying, my thoughts cannot escape me, they are held as I am held, they understand very well.

He says at last, he has been talking for a very long time, talking, commanding, expostulating, commanding, I cannot resist and I am getting you know a little bit, how is it? I do not wish to be off at all now, I am a very willing captive to all that he is saying, it rings a bell inside of my head and of my heart, I am really very contained, now, very practical, alert, and I am becoming excited and wishing to laugh out loud, it is a relief to me what he is saying, it is a direct orientation of my thought, a relief, an orientation, an éclaircissement, a something that makes me want to stand up and shout I am so glad.

He echoes my own thoughts.

'Oh Pompey, to hell with the tea parties and the tea-tattle and chère Josephine and chère chère Haidée that made you so cross, there was never anyone so cross, do you know how cross you were when first you came to Schloss Tilssen, so cross so cross, and all the time so desperately, but quite desperately not there. But you began to notice didn't you? Eh? You noticed old Peck, he drove you nearly frantic, didn't he? With that absentminded night-wandering of his, his eternally mislaid spectacle case, his ne plus ultra of a 'Not here I fear' that drove you running mad into the night to take also Josephine and Haidée and go sailing sailing up the Baltic to the far north up and away towards Lapland in a frantic search for an end to it all? This is true, isn't it Pompey, answer me?'

He drops my hands and takes me by the shoulders, shaking me gently, for my eyes have gone dark again and the thoughts are straining straining to be away in the boat, away in our sweet *Baranar* 2 to go flying upon the dark cold waters, north and north again.

'Pompey, answer me.' He shakes me not so gently, and calls more loudly, 'Pompey, come back. Pompey!' He forces me to look at him, to stare into his eyes, oddly lighted, light and ferocious in the light of the high full moon, shining down from above the light is thrown up again from the sea, is thrown up from the surf and shining phosphorescent water, to shine again in the eyes of this exigeant Major Satterthwaite.

'Yes,' I say, dully, tiredly, I am now getting so-o-o tired, it is amazing how suddenly I am become but quite . . . 'Yes, I remember everything, I have forgotten nothing.'

'And those little journeys of yours into Ool,' he is

laughing again, 'so it was not all sweet feminine companionship, eh? not all the tea-tattle and the long picnics in the sunshine, and bathing with Haidée and carrying baby Reine out beyond the surf to drop her plomp into some safe pool left by the high tide high above the dangerous open sea currents, no it was not all this, was it? Answer me.'

'No, it was not all this. And suppose now, for instance, what else do you know?' I am laughing too, and a little mocking this suddenly-so-intelligent British officer. 'What else, Tom?'

'Your visits to that un-Christian friend of yours in Ool – that charming little share-pusher, old Aaronsen in Margaretenstrasse, eh? What price nitrates now, eh Pompey?'

I laugh. 'Why they've dropped 20 points my dear, that is the position as it stands at the moment.'

'And you're holding on, you're not selling, you're holding on for a rise, old Aaronsen put you on to that, it isn't altogether a speculation, is it?'

'Old Aaronsen is a very wise old bird, and the only intelligent person I have met since I came this way.'

'Not excepting me?' says Tom, mocking in his turn.

'*Now* not excepting you – I mean now not including you, I mean now excepting you, my dear, and perhaps that clever Colonel Peck too.' I am laughing again. It is a blind man's buff we have been playing and now I am rather glad you know that it has not got to be played any more, it was getting rather tiresome, rather boring, rather puzzling too for me, for they could not have been quite so silly, and even now. . . .

'What *do* you know about Aaronsen, Tom?'

'I like him, I rather respect him, I agree, gracious Miss, that he is easily and without making any effort to stretch himself at all, quite the most intelligent person in Ool – and that is excepting nobody, not that boiled owl of a University Herr Professor Direcktor God-Knows-What of theirs, and certainly not excepting the retired Herr General Military Instructor and certainly oh certainly not excepting the highly inflammable student material they are shaping to what calamity we can guess. Oh we can guess very well, clever people like you and me, and Peck and Aaronsen, eh?'

We both laugh, but he is really charming, but charming this handsome Tom, whose handsomeness even I had got to forget and whose forced banality of conversation I was only just beginning to suspect.

He is talking again and I listen very carefully, very seriously.

He is saying . . . 'You can be immensely useful to Peck and me, Pompey. You will, won't you? You will, and you won't forget, and you will for once be a good girl and remember and remember all the time, and not just now and then as the fit takes you, Promise?'

He pulls me to my feet, and we go running running back to the Schloss. It is very late now, late for the invalids of the Schloss to be running and conspiring and laughing with midnight upon the air. We hurried back, racing through the undergrowth and out on to the wide grass rides so soft and dark in the shadow of the pine trees. Schloss Tilssen did not give us a welcome, it was too late, no, really, we were offside of the unwritten curfew laws that no man, and no woman, shall crash through the undergrowth of the pine woods so late, so late at night, to come racing and running up to the very front doors of this ancient and severe establishment.

For almost you know we were upon a Kurhaus regime, where all is done so severely, so practically, for the good of the inmates, and so much against their wishes that indeed it is the nanny-tale all over again, why it is so beastly boring, so fatiguing so enervating and in every way so enormously inconvenient, why it must be good for you, there is nothing else it can be but that.

But do not imagine that there is anyone (that we have found) at the Schloss to enforce this ineffable nanny-rule upon the delicate cross child that already in pain and weakness and an impotent great fury is turning this way and that against a coercion that it cannot break or stretch or indeed in any way do anything but suffer. But at the Schloss there is a delicate Gefühl that is more strong than strong, and has us all within its stretch, against our will if we are sensitive to be aware of its existence, against our consciousness, for the most part, for the most part it is against our consciousness. But it is strong to constrain *for the cross child's good*, so that sometimes coming home tired of an evening, from riding or shooting with this dear Tom, from picnics and swimming parties with chère Josephine and the Baronin, it is a burden, conscious or unconscious upon our thought, to drink the hot milk and go quickly to bed. For this purpose is dinner very early served at this Schloss. Seven o'clock sees us set down to the simplest of dinners that is indeed hardly to be dignified by that name, suggestive of social occasion and the first of long hours of distraction. But for us it is the end of the day and not the beginning of the evening with night hot upon it, and the long swift hours of intercourse upon occasion. Midnight is the latest last stretch of our coercion, and however happily sailing upon the sea under the high moon, up and ever upwards along the coast, with this longing and seeking for the last limits of imagined Lapland, homewards we have turned, tacking against the wind, to beach our boat, our darling *Baranar* 2, and leave it with sails folded upon oars within the boat house, to reach the great doorway of the Schloss *not later than midnight*, so nanny-minded are we, so obedient.

But now did I say it was midnight? Why it is long past that hour I thought was striking even now upon us, running up the steps towards the kitchen entrance, since the portals frown upon us and will have none of our adventures.

'Why, Tom, it is later than I thought.'

'Well, my dear, it is two o'clock to be precise.'

'But where have we been all this time, where have the hours gone, for certainly it was not so late when in a great fury of fear and dis-ease I came running out of the great drawing-room to sit on the cliff top and think?'

Tom takes my arm. 'Do not worry about that, Pompey, why you have been talking for hours, for hours. My dear, you had lost all sense of time.'

'But have *I* been talking? But I thought it was you, why it was you, why Tom, it was you that was telling me, and telling me, and questioning and asking why it was certainly you and not I at all.'

Tom laughs. We have broken in now through the little pantry door and are coming up the steps to the large wide low-roofed kitchen.

'You have told me more than you imagine, Pompey, and very glad I was to hear it, and am, and am.' He laughs again but suddenly puts his hand to my lips and pulls me back into the shadow of the stairway. There is a light in the kitchen that we did not switch on, there is somebody there perhaps, it looks a little dangerous. I strain forward again, I am rather curious, who is this who is in the further room, it is rather unearthly too, I am getting rather frightened and excited, it is like when I was a child we used to play this game, to become enormously frightened, to be so terrified we must run out of the great house, we could not bear for another moment to be inside of it. And the password to that anarchy of the imagination was this and only this, whispered in a *concealing* matter of factness of tone, with all of the delicious excitement of fear lambent beneath it: *Did you hear anything?*

And now, Did I hear anything? Yes, I heard the scratch-scratch of a fine pen-nib travelling rather slowly, rather careful-careful, upon the surface of some rather bad quality notepaper I should think, for it travels and pauses and splutters, and then there is a pause while perhaps the too-much of ink is shaken on to the blotting-paper, and then the scratch-scratch begins again, and there is a cough and a sniff and the little human noises. Shall I imagine a writer who is conscientious to get everything down on to the paper well spelt and right, but who has not any great natural talent for putting thought into words? But perhaps I am quite wrong. Perhaps this slowness and this scratch-scratch is the arduous labour of copying from one sheet of paper to another? Perhaps it is that? Or perhaps it is not in simple English at all, but in some, to the writer, foreign language, or code. Or code?

How romantic and melodramatic is Pompey at midnight and two hours past. But I am naturally code-minded, dear Reader, for all of that that I have had to do with the dear and distant baronet, in my office in London not for secrecy and melodrama here but for cheapness. And oh no, except in some ways perhaps, oh yes. For secrecy in many communications of financial importance is so necessary, and native clerks in mining areas are not above a price that is not above the worth-while sturdy consideration of an oh-so-practical fellow-magnate. When shares are to be held or sold or pooled or halved and when rumour is strong upon the wing, secrecy is of paramount importance, and when So-and-So will bring himself to be such an obstinate and unaccommodating idiot, oh there is no end to it all. For remember, my chicks, capitalism is not only wrong, it is also very difficult.

Very difficult and exasperating indeed is this capitalismus toil that has in it all of the exasperating deviations and incalculabilities of the human factor, that goes to make it in its practical every-day application so much so very much more difficult and exasperating than the simple straightforwardness of the abstractions upon a theme that is all that there is of all that there is of Monsieur Karl.

For in the *pratique* of capitalismus indeed there is so very much of this exasperating and so-human incalculability that grates upon tempers and leads to the association of incongruous personalities with nothing to link them together but that famous Board Room table where baronet and lord, Empire-Blue-Eyes and Israel, come to have so much of agacement in the pursuit of dividends.

And now I am laughing a little, for my thoughts go off to centre again upon that Sir I-Name-No-Names who was one of the most tormented exasperated and frustrated of all financiers I have ever met; who desired nothing but the good health of his dividends but nothing but this and only this; and is not this just a little thing to want and to work for, to put his whole shoulder to the wheel and to be a sacrifice of all of the natural affections and simple home ties? Oh indeed his martyrdom was heavy upon him, and heavy indeed upon the ears of so many as were so unfortunate to fall in with him to have to listen. Oh but what an abominable bore the man is. Oh how can he come to say it and to say it again and again? But he is nearly in tears, but these dividends. . . . It is sad for him, it is certainly sad that people will not understand that in the pellucid depths of his coeur d'enfant there is not one thought but for the good of others, for the good of others, of for instance these little dividends, that by now cannot I think, for all his sobs and tears and the wringing of hands and high hysteria of abandon, be quite so quite so altogether little? But now, he says, and it is the high moment of his crucifixion, But now I cannot, indeed I *will not* have these details circulated to the shareholders. For all of them are ladies of no previous business experience.

Oh how I love that expression, oh how rich and full and entirely glorious it is. You see? He has been so far so successful that he has placed his share-holding with these so-naive ladies, do you know I think they are the ladies who are the dream of every company promoter's child-heart of love and longing. These are the ladies, I make no bones, who will support any venture provided it has to do with something that is *getting rather dangerous.* Do you see? They have a tendre for tramway companies in distant lands where, if they can have it this way too, please, already the tramway system is about to be ousted by a motor bus company. And the funny thing is, and very soon they will come to find it out, the tramway company will be eaten up by this bus company, but what they will never come to find out (for the financiers in their kindness will keep it from them) is just this, that just this Sir Nameless is both bus and tram company that takes over from himself. Why, it is so simple. Why there is no offence at all. If you have experience – it is so simple. But the naive ladies will just say: Oh those tramways? Oh that was unfortunate, yes, but it was unfortunate. And they will then have their martyrdom too, it will be heavy upon them. But for Sir Nameless his martyrdom is only perhaps for him so much of a burden because it is rather difficult, really it is impossible . . . why to suggest that information should be circulated to shareholders *who are these ladies of no previous business experience*. . . .

Oh I very much prefer the noble and exhilarating Topheim who said, well somebody said to him: Well look here Topheim, you haven't done so badly out of this yourself. And what said Topheim of the ready answer, of the pat back upon pat? I'm not meant to do badly out of it, said the sweet boy. I said, I'm not meant to do badly out of it.

So all of this has been my song in far-off England, and is it then to be a matter of surprise that standing under cover to hear the scratch-scratch of the secret writer at this unchristian hour of the early dark morning, my thoughts travel code-ward bearing with them the trappings of financial interest that here I guess that here I guess that is not here.

So I strain, I pull, I will go forward to see who it is who is sitting in the room writing, writing. But

Tom pulls me back, he will have none of it, but, taller than I, can see no doubt can see who sits within, can see and keep it to himself.

But he is right to keep me back, for presently the writing ceases, and there is a shuffle of papers to be blotted and gathered up in a neat pile, and there is all this for some seconds, and now there is a frou-frou of skirts, it is a woman then, and footsteps retreating through the room, and the further door opens and suddenly it is quite dark in the kitchen, the light has been switched off, the midnight-late writer is to her room departed. 'Even here is a season of rest, And I to my cabin repair.' Yes I guess that now-and-about-time-too she is to her cabin repaired.

It is deliciously exciting. We will give her five minutes. We sit on the floor waiting waiting for the cautionary five minutes to pass. I rest my head against the stair rail and think that very soon it will be more exciting, but now it is a little boring, but very soon it will be more exciting, and very soon after that I shall be able to go to bed. I am very tired, I am feeling rather disembodied and yet rather feverishly excited. Tom flashes his torch into my face again and in the reflected light his own face looks drawn and pale and rather worried, poor Tom, this worry now I hear him speak, it is for me. He puts his arm round me and pulls me forward so that my head is bent downwards and not lying stretched back against the stairs.

'Poor Pompey, you will soon be in bed now. Just another few minutes and then we can go, and to-morrow stay in bed until after lunch. I'll come and knock on your door about tea time. That is better, isn't it, that sounds nice, eh? Let me see it's Wednesday now, Thursday, a nice long sleep in bed for you, my dear, and Friday . . . and Saturday, by Saturday we shall be across the frontier.'

This is perfectly sensible to me, but I am now so tired and stupid it is not set out precisely in my consciousness.

'And Friday, Friday?' I say, so tired, so very tired and stupid.

'Friday you must see Aaronsen about the draft on New York. That Pompey is Friday's business, and you will want all your wits about you. And now I think we can go and have a look at Mrs. Pouncer's blotting-paper.'

'Pouncer? Then it was Pouncer that was writing there . . . Pouncer?'

Tom laughs. 'I'm sorry I couldn't let you into the secret, but I am not so sure she is as deaf as she makes out, and you were making the most infernal little bit of a rustle weren't you? There would have been some bunny-fluff flying if she'd got wind of it, and we don't want that.'

Tom torch-lights himself across the kitchen and switches the lights on. I run to the table. Yes, this is my pigeon. There is not one scrap of paper left to tell a tale, and little but boring cross-hatchings on the white blotting-paper. But there is one clear impression of several words together on a line. I take the mirror from my handbag and look at it, I look at this so intriguing writing that is now clearly to be read in my looking-glass world. I laugh and laugh, it is so funny, and read it out to Tom who is now leaning over my shoulder.

'Issue of troops to blankets.'

Quickly I take some old envelope from my bag and write on it with the pen and ink that are on the table, and blot it beneath the clear impression on the blotting-paper and hold it up for Tom to read, that now reads altogether, that now reads and I must read it out aloud:

'Issue of troops to blankets.'

'Keep away from the bottle, I said Keep away from the bottle, I said.'

'That,' says Tom, 'is the correct answer. Darling, you are wonderful.' He kisses the top of my head. Deceitful Tom, is he laughing up there, I cannot see, and my looking glass has clouded over, my looking-glass world is for this moment, it has to be, for this necessary moment, obscured. So is he laughing, or is he laughing, I do not know.

So Pouncer is in it too, so she is, is she? But Tom is laughing now and his voice seems to come from some long way off, though I am standing up and he is holding me by the arms.

'Oh yes, she's in it, my dear, she is very decidedly in it, but on which side, on which side?'

So we switch the lights off and go upstairs laughing, laughing so much, it is really such an extremely good joke, this Pouncer joke.

Night life at the Schloss is certainly very interesting and exhilarating and on the long view very funny-ha-ha indeed, for there is a lot to be learnt from the shadows that come sloping across from the pantry and from the words that are blotted upon the copy.

How nice it is to stay in bed on a cold October day when the damp ground-fog is seeping up from the inland sea and from the coast line upon the village and up the streets and in at my open window. Josephine has decided to have breakfast in bed with me. We have the pillows piled up behind us; it is very comfortable and the fire is a wood fire that burns furiously on the hearth and throws out a very comforting heat and light.

'Pompey, you have had a night out, you look frightful, but my dear you should not have these late nights, they are making you ill again. But I heard you come up to bed last night, I was awake and I heard you run past my door and I heard you open your door and shut it after you. It is no use denying it, I know it was you, and you know I think it is awfully unwise of you, I say nothing about running round with Tom so late at night, I say nothing about that, that is your own affair, but what I do say is this, it is awfully silly of you to be so late. You have no sense of time at all, you are so awfully absent minded, I have often noticed it in you, it makes a lot of trouble for other people; now I don't say that I mind, I don't, but I do say, how often you have been for instance quite impossibly late for lunch, always we are having to keep the lunch back for you, when you are staying with me at . . . (this little seaside town on the south coast of England is now in Josephine's mind). It is quite all right with me, so far as I personally am concerned I do not mind at all sitting waiting for lunch until perhaps half past two, and if the lunch is by that time cold, no, I do not mind, it makes no difference to me at all, I am accustomed to it, my aunt for instance when she is staying with me has no consideration whatever for the servants. She could never keep any of her own for more than a week, after that week they went, and nothing she could do was of any use to make them stay, and I cannot altogether blame them, because, although I think that maids as a class are quite without any consideration at all, but are just out for all that they can get, without anything of loyalty or consideration for their employers at all, here, I think, they had something to make them not wish to stay another minute in my aunt's house. For there is nothing like unpunctuality and constant lateness to lunch and dinner to make trouble for the maids, but I say nothing about that, only I cannot help remembering, I am not cross, but I cannot help remembering one day, you were out on the cliffs, and lunch was at one o'clock and we kept the lunch . . .'

'Josephine,' I cry, 'Josephine, it is true that that happened once, once, and certainly now I think you have remembered it all very well to tell it again with so much of empressement. But once it happened. Once. And that was when I got bogged on your abominable cliffs so that hardly did I come out alive from that abominable red clay bog that had got up already above the tops of my wellington boots.'

'Nanny's wellington boots, if I might just interrupt you for one moment, darling,' said Josephine, looking at me triumphantly above the egg-spoon poised half-way to lip.

Touchée, touchée. I am now quite touchée and extinct. I have nothing to say. Victory on all points to Josephine. We are now ready to talk about something else. It is this. We are to have a grand party on Friday night. On Friday night . . . but surely Friday, was there not something else to be done on

Friday? I cannot remember. So I throw this something that is already nothing I throw it to the winds and I am all Josephine's to talk about this grand party and arrange, and arrange. For Josephine is a tiger for arrangement, and a very good and efficient tiger indeed. We are to have, there is this and that, and we are to have a very slap-up and un-invalidish and very contra-Schloss *late* dinner. It is set for half-past-eight. Seven o'clock? Oh that is too enervating, too childish and ridiculous. No, it is to be set for half-past-eight. And we are all to dress up in our very best clothes, and the men are to be forced to dress too, and it is to be a party, and there is to be music and dancing after dinner.

'But dancing, Josephine, will Mrs. Pouncer and the old ladies will they dance?' Oh but that does not matter, they can dance if they like, or they can sit and look on, but we shall dance, and Colonel Peck must dance, and Tom, and Haidée's Baron is coming at Friday lunchtime for the weekend and he must dance too, we are to show the Baron what we can do.

'Haidée and I will arrange it all, Pompey, you had better stay in bed and sleep, because you really look quite unearthly my pet, and you must stay in bed and sleep it off, and if you will be so silly to stay out so late, no I do not think it is at all a good thing, and I'm quite sure if *They* realized, they would be quite but absolutely furious.'

This so-oblique way of referring to the Schloss-atmosphere, that restraining constraining nanny-atmosphere, is a little bit curious, and to me a little bit also alarming. It lines up in my mind with the thought I have had about this What will they think of next. The atmosphere is then a plurality, a plurality of benevolent constraint, and if met by opposition, how benevolent, ah how benevolent — and how constraining?

Josephine jumps out of bed and runs to the looking glass.

'Josephine you can have that Thamar lotion of mine, do put it on and see how you look, it is awfully good by artificial light, turn the light on, it is really quite dark and foggy enough to get the effect.'

Josephine carefully does her face, sitting in the low chair before the mirror. Darken your eye-lashes, darling, I cry.

With expert quick fingers Josephine applies the cosmetic.

'You look ravishing. Colonel Peck will be seduced. You must be kind to Colonel Peck, Josephine, and you must not be too seducing: it is a little bit more than he is up to I guess.'

Josephine is telling me the story of the vicar of Nontwich. His wife had white eyelashes so it is easy to see why she must tell me the story of the vicar of Nontwich. She and Jamie and he and his wife were playing golf. But Josephine was furious that day, she was quite ravingly furious. And Jamie missed all his putts and hooked all his drives. And there was only Josephine to stand between them and the bitterness of defeat. So alas and alas, because Josephine now must have the misfortune also to hook her drive, that sends the ball whizzing whizzing off the fairway into the treacherous rough undergrowth. And the vicar would not help her look for it. I guess he was a tired old man and there was his wife that had the white eyelashes to be a burden upon his old age. So the vicar and I sat quietly upon a bunker and Jamie and Josephine beat up the undergrowth, and so it went on until the vicar in the innocence of his mild heart must suggest that Josephine put down another ball. Oh but this was the uttermost last insult and atrocious treachery. Put down another ball, and lose a stroke, oh what a piece of heartless impudence. No one but a vicar of high church tendency could have thought for one moment to make such a monstrous suggestion — so sly, so wily, this sly and wily priest, and up to no good with his reserved sacrament and the way he would not play tennis.

'But Josephine, he had lumbago so badly, it was sad for him, how could he for instance with this lumbago of his come to play tennis at the village club?'

'If he wanted to, Pompey, he could have done it

well enough. In the end he had to apply for another living. His wife, you know, and then, and then . . . Dr. Gumbit told me about it. You wouldn't understand . . . He was ostracized by the entire choir. Look Pompey, does that look all right?' 'Oh Josephine you look exactly like Cynthia Crale.' Josephine laughs and does a slight prance round the room further to suggest the enterprising Cynthia whose private life . . . whose private life. . . .

But Josephine is as strong as a lion to have and hold and not to go seeking and hoping in a fury of unreason, and if now in a frivolous moment her thought is for the telling application of make-up and the thorough exploitation of a beauty-potterismus that is rather foreign to her habit, it is only for the moment for this amusing moment of my day-in-bed.

I jump out of bed, I am getting rather bored really lying here so very wide awake, and I slip on my dressing-gown and slippers.

'Pompey,' cries Josephine, 'what are you doing? Get back to bed at once.'

The authoritative fundamental Josephine breaks through the Cynthia-mask with a rather comic effect.

'Oh no I really won't, I should be too bored, I really find it boring to lie here so wide awake. Come on Josephine, let's go and visit Mrs. Pouncer and tell her about the party, she always has her breakfast sent up to her room and it will be amusing to go and see this extremely mysterious and fascinating old lady, yes we will do that, it will be good for me, it will be the change the doctors were so unanimous to recommend for me.'

'You and your old Pouncer! Why Pompey I believe you have a really vicious passion for this old girl.'

We run along the corridor and knock on the door.

'Come in,' trills the pretty voice of Pouncer, so in we go.

Pouncer is sitting up in bed looking truly magnificent. Her wig, yes I think now it has to be a wig, is looking très dandy, and her face has a freshly enamelled look that is rather appealing in its sense of formalism, to be so well enamelled so early in the morning, that is very admirable, I find it very admirable indeed to be so chic at half-past-eleven in the morning. She has her ear trumpet well a-cock for news.

'We are going to give a party on Friday evening.' Josephine and I shout in unison.

'Friday evening?' The Pouncer looks at me a little mockingly, very intent.

'You are running it rather close aren't you my dear?' She says this to me. Josephine looks like she thought it was all up, all up and over with what few poor wits the old girl had. But the next sentence of Mrs. Pouncer is indeed to give the coup de grâce to

Josephine's thoughts about the thoughts of the old girl that sits up in bed so spry and so elegant.

'Why does the American Count drink so much?'

Josephine is edging towards the door. I guess she has all my detestation for mental derangement in all its varieties of eccentricity. But there is more to it than this, I know indeed, in my dark heart of increasing fear and of half-apprehended surmise, I know indeed.

You witch, Pouncer, I think, you witch, and rather I think too, You devil-witch, you hell's brew of a sly old widow. And I say, without overmuch thinking, I say by instinct:

'I guess the blotting-paper was thirsty, I guess it was thirsty.'

And I remember this grand blotting-paper that is called by this grand name: *The American Count*, and I am laughing a little to think and remember what I had forgotten for the moment to remember, how this grand blotting-paper is the superbly grand victory that came from the grand fuss-up that Colonel Peck made to the management of our Schloss in a fury of excessive indignation for the poor quality of the then existing (and since how long) blotting-pads in the writing rooms of the Schloss. So in the final upshot, and after the reverberations of this magnificent fury of Colonel Peck had a little diminished, look one day if we did not find neat and padded within its leather corners such a magnificent blotting arrangement, so rich in colour and powerful in absorbence that we could not for one moment have envisaged – not the Colonel Peck himself.

And round its luxurious bulk, to show the mark and patent of its virginity was bound a strip of manufacturer's glazed paper to bear the name that has been for all the peevish guests of the Schloss a bond for a good joke '*The American Count*'.

What Vatican occasion had ennobled what son of Old Glory I do not know, but very excellent was his manufactury, so much so that for a long time afterwards we were reluctant to blot our letters upon it, and even the Colonel had the atmosphere of being a little pink about the ears to have had so much of unpleasantness met by so much of magnanimity.

I guess the blotting-paper was thirsty the night I sat with Tom to blot the raw joke of the Keep-away-from-the-bottle idea beneath the crazy wording of Pouncer's imprint. I guess the blotting-paper was thirsty.

Josephine has by now quite edged away from us and out of the room into sanity and security. My poor Pompey, I can do no more for you, her last look to me has said. And indeed she can do nothing but nothing at all. She is right to have gone.

My eyes are very withdrawn, remote and sad, and I look at this famous Mrs. Pouncer, this rich Old

Girl, with her compelling force of inquisition undertoning the plastered elegance.

If you have anything in you of pride and ambition . . . She says this, she says this to me. Oh what have I not in me of pride and ambition to make a misery and a darkness in my heart, and are there no tears, and is there no anger. Ah, how this dark moment moves me, yes it touches to my very heart of fury, to the heart of the heart of this occasion.

But I will give the answer that I must give, that I must give, this answer, the words that are already upon my lips. And let confusion riot and come what may, we are set for this thing now. 'I know to what bad things I go, but louder than all wrath doth cry, Anger that maketh man's worst misery.' The translation, dear Reader, is not my own, having indeed upon it all of the incidence of sentimentality of this kind Grecian. But it serves, it serves, for in my heart this great fury is rising like a high wind that draws strongly from the north, to carry before it all of the lesser emotions of fear and bewilderment and of childish elation of excitement. So my lips frame the words and I say the words in the tonal dullness of a learnt lesson: I say . . .

The words fall from me without the collusion of my mind; I am innocent of their significance. But Pouncer is delighted, but she is quite and absolutely enchanted.

'My dear Pompey,' she cries. 'My dear Pompey!' Her face breaks beneath the points of a hundred splintered smiles; it is the mirror of Kay, it is all of the splinters of that frozen mirror in this smiling smiling face. The effect of the gaiety of this smile – so gay, so gay is the Pouncer at this moment, it has something in it, it has something in it do you know, of the absolutely appalling. And it is so infectious, in the character of this appalling gaiety there is a compelling strength, so that I laugh too, smiling, smiling and ceremoniously bowing and smiling, I stand by her bedside, with something too of an oriental politeness in my gentle obsequious laughter. I am basking in the light of a false fire, a fata morgana, aha Pouncer, what of an Eulenspiegel is there in you, my dear Mrs. Witch?

I stand beside her bed, and now she has been talking to me for hours it seems, and her voice runs on and my thoughts go with it in a way that is not perhaps entirely usual with me, but now I am completely fascinated and held, there is the spell of this fine voice that goes to send the words above my head, falling to my feet and pointing upwards to a heart that was too secret. I am fascinated and held and lifted up and out of my dark moment into a pure exaltation that has nothing in it of mortality. And the voice goes on and the quick running magic goes with it and my thoughts go too, for I am enchanted and ravished out of myself by this sweet voice that has made for me this time-pocket of a quiet happiness. But I have in me all the weight cloths of mortality to point the thought that comes now to break this spell, as the Pouncer in her mortality has no doubt wished it should; and feeling it upon the wing I must cry to the flying moment, Stay, so fair thou art. And so it is upon the wind and out of the window at once, or up the chimney, since it was perhaps for all its sweet enchantment a witch's moment and nothing more than this.

I am so tired now, and rather drowsy, and happy still with the quiet singing happiness of the fled moment, I am drowsy and happy and there is a singing sound in my ears. It is like I was lying upon the hills above Ravenscar, lying in the heather upon a hot summer's day, when there is this time pause and all of eternity for your hands to hold. And the sky is so blue and so distant, and in the depths of that blue sky there is this singing-singing, where the air is so enchanting, so buoyant and ethereal, it is the singing-singing in your ears of a pleasant death-note, that shall be repeated once again to make an end forever.

Pouncer lays her hand upon my hand.

'If there is anything in you of pride and ambition, Pompey, you must do well. Late at night on Friday you will ride off with your escort . . .' (she cannot bring herself then to pronounce the name of my dear Tom?) 'and that will be the beginning, for you that will be the beginning. And later you will go again, and again, and perhaps you will go alone; but be sure you do well, be sure you do very well.' She smiles a little, measuring up to the pride and ambition that are stirring out of sleep in my heart. 'Do well, do well.' She is looking very seriously out of the window for the moment and withdraws her hand from mine. 'There will be winter in the air', her head is turned away, I can hardly hear her any longer. 'There will be winter in the air, and death in winter upon the wind from the north. Do well, do well. . . .'

I go back to my room now and the windows are flung wide open to stand folded back upon the little iron balcony. I get into bed and fall asleep. A very deep sleep, it is such a beautiful sleep, so dark and complete, it is the most enchanting sleep. And I am at last awoken by the knocking on the door, and it is Tom to bring my tea upon a tray.

But Friday's business comes with Friday, and it is morning, and in the crisp October air I ride through the woods over towards Ool to see

Aaronsen about this draft on New York, for it has all become clear in my mind now, and I have no doubt that I shall obtain my dollar bill at a good exchange.

Aaronsen receives me in his large low room on the first floor. This runs across the whole width of the house and has french windows at either end. There is a grand piano at the garden window and there are tall vases with magnolias at stand about the room.

Aaronsen is delighted to see me and to tell the truth I am delighted to see him, for I admire this old Jew and by now we are great friends. He has coffee and rich cream cakes for me, but himself he does not take anything for he is dyspeptic and thank heavens, I think to myself, eating into my second cake, and helping my coffee to another spoonful of cream, thank heavens I am not.

Now he sits down at the piano to play some Chopin. He is partial to Chopin is Aaronsen, and as the melancholy sweet music of *Les Sylphides* falls upon the silence of the room, I think I am too, yes I think that I am also partial to Chopin. It is delightful here, there is a feeling of sophistication that is rather perhaps an old fashioned sophistication of old fashioned pre-war cultured society circles in Vienna or St. Petersburg.

My father knew St. Petersburg well in the days

of long ago when it was St. Petersburg or Petersburg (in the way that it was Petersburg, as Johannesburg is Joburg, to its friends and intimates), and this is what makes me think of Petersburg to put it in here.

Very essentially civilized, urbane and international, in this sweet sweet cultured sentimental manner, that is so what Allemagne barbare detests, is this old Jew Aaronsen. And very easily I find myself slipping into his mood that does not come at all foreign to me. *Barbare* is always so foreign to me, you know, it rouses in me such a fury to destroy, to be so cruel, with more than battle cruelty, to be so cruel to tread upon the ecstatic face of this idealismus barbarus, that it takes me out of my rhythm in a way that I do not at all like, in the way that goes to make me still more destroyingly furious.

Ah the Zurückkehren of the barbarismus oh the Blödsinnigkeit of the idealismus, that is all of what cher Aaronsen is not.

But in permitting myself to become so destroyingly furious and so intolerant, is it not to find in myself a little of this very barbarismus I so much should like to wipe out for all time from all people? No, I do not think this in me, and in those who feel as I do, is barbarismus, intolerance yes, but it is the sharp spear of defence against infamy that must bear for a sharp point the uttermost sharp point of a righteous pure intolerance.

Aaronsen and I have often discussed the perils and provocations of idealismus in the abstract, attached, for the sake of discussion, to no cause, good to our thinking or evil. And we have come to see that we feel much the same about it, and it is for us a bond that ties us together, and makes for me these quiet happy hours with my cream cakes and creamed coffee in the little tinkling Meissen cups, and for him the pleasure of a shared pleasure in the Chopin sounds that spring to life beneath his gifted fingers. For the boy is a good pianist, make no mistake, very delicate and precise is his fingering, and very aloof his manner, so that what there is of sentimentality is what there is of sentimentality in Chopin and has no contributory cause within the player of these sad sweet sounds.

Ah poor Jew, what he and his race have brought upon their heads in the practice of and flight from a mutually incongruous idealismus. 'Only the Jews would have survived their persecutions.' Another gloss. Only a people hungry and ripe for persecution would have inspired and survived such a history. Did not Christ himself, encouraging and embracing his death upon the cross, set the pace for future sad heroic ages of dissent? Sacrifice to the gods, a pinch of salt, a pinch of salt. And our pregnant and familiar gloss of this most tragic pause. Take it with a pinch of salt. Ah what then? For if the early Christians had indeed taken all of their religion and the Romans' with just this pinch of salt, thereby with a mighty spear-thrust of derision and pride in human pride, cutting to the heart of all persecuting and persecuted idealismus, what then? For have not the Christian Churches themselves shown us (with a candour we were too foolish to apprise) the dangers to an established hierarchy of just this lip service that only the Romans in a practical cynicism could accept? Ah what a weapon they put into our hands, that we did not use, we did not use. Ah past ages, what crime is yours, what cruelty and folly, that this so-powerful and indicated weapon you did not use, you did not use. When the founder of your Church Himself has said: He who is not for me is against me, and in the divinity of His unhappiness, in the despair of the depths of the stupidity of the indifference, turning at last to that most bitter death, to cry aloud in the uttermost abandonment of His despair 'Je me débarasse de la vie'.

Oh how much of the splendour of torment and dismay is wrecked and splintered upon the seas of our ideas, not held to be discussed in a reasonable quietude, to be measured in a proud humility against a common thought, but thrust, thrust to the hilt of its destroying fury and dyed deep with the insensate blood of a too willing martyrarchy. Scatter the salt before the Roman gods, acquiesce in the uttermost fantastic formularies of the inquisition, ratify the amendments, sign the protocols, scatter, acquiesce, ratify and sign, but keep your heart to yourself for a space to laugh in, for not the most searching pang can strip naked that inmost core of laughter within a secret heart, that holds fierce and close within itself the power to dispel the dream, the dream that persecutes and is persecuted, *the dream that slew the slayer and shall be slain.* Slain? By no avowed slayer, bringing death upon himself, but slain, slain and finally slain by the laughter behind an acquiescence that mocks and kills.

I am getting a little restless now. I have finished my coffee and licked the last crumb of the last cream cake from my finger tips, but still the sweet sad sound is on the air, and Aaronsen in some far distant place of withdrawal plays and plays, and the notes are too plaintive, too insistent, they cry to me with the extreme streng h and tenacity of an appeal. I am very restless and I walk to the street window and look down into the street. The house gives directly on to the market square of Ool; there is quite a small crowd surging upon the pavement below. I step on to the balcony and look below. My eyes meet the upturned faces, furious and rather surprised, of a group of students from the little university. No doubt they were expecting Aaronsen, and no doubt they had some catcalls ready for him.

But the foreign lady, for they must know me by now, I have so often strolled about their streets with Josephine and Reine, and ridden through the town with Tom, puts them a little aback, and they whisper and whisper and at last move off. All the same they were looking rather threatening.

I come back into the room and call to Aaronsen to awaken him from his *Chopin-manie*. We get down at once, dear Reader, to tacks. To tacks. The draft business is quickly arranged, it is rather a large sum that is to go through Morgenbaum of New York, but the ultimate payees, I need hardly say, (well need I? – certainly not to Aaronsen), are Birdie, Birdie, Strand and Dolland of an address that is rather nearer our homes, yours and mine.

'And now my dear,' says Aaronsen, 'I have some good news for you. We have been very successful with your nitrates, I have made quite a packet for you. Gluckmann wired just in time and I sold at the peak.'

'How much?' I say.

He names a sum that is certainly quite impressive. I am not meant to do badly out of it (dear Topheim), well certainly I have not.

'What do you want done with the money – you'll need some of it pretty soon I suppose?'

'Good God no, not a cent,' I say. I am profoundly

shocked at the thought that I should spend my own money on this venture into which I have been, though excitingly, rather more than less shanghaied.

'That's splendid, my dear,' says Aaronsen. 'The best soldiers are mercenaries.'

We drink a glass of kirschwasser to my success.

'If there's any trouble, Aaron, you'd better get out early.'

But no, he is adamant, he will not leave, he is devoted to the appearance of this little town of Ool, which certainly has great charm if only its inhabitants were not so damn-all stupid.

'I guess you are easily the wisest person here, but I'd sooner see you safe in London.'

A very secretive and very obstinate look comes upon his old face. No, he will not go, I know it is useless, he will not go. They never will.

'Well we're sure to win, I don't say we're not, we've more money, better material, better brains. But much good that will do you sitting here with your throat slit, my poor Aaron. Well, think it over, think it over. If you change your mind, Tom will countersign your papers and you can leave when you like. You've been extremely good to us and we shan't forget it. I shan't at any rate.'

For a tired expression of good-humoured doubt has come into Aaronsen's eyes. It is something no doubt, these rather official pompous words of mine are something that I dare say he has heard before.

I repeat: 'I shan't at any rate.' And I go up to him and take him by the hand and I smile up into his face. I like him so much, he is in many ways so admirable. I ask him to come to the party Josephine and Haidée and I are giving in the evening. He is at once tremendously pleased.

'I know that you won't forget, Pompey, but I think that your remembering will not have very much power to help me, but I know that you will not forget.'

He smiles down upon me, there is a haze of friendship and good-bye in the air. I am almost crying, I like him so much and the good-bye is in the air.

'Don't think me a screw and a prig, dear Aaron,' I say. He has been so kind, and the only intelligent person, yes the only really intelligent person, to be urbane and many-sided and sensible, that I have met since leaving London.

'No, Pompey, you are not a prig. And as for the screw. Well it was a close bargain you drove, but the screw business as you call it, I must admire you for that, my nose makes me have to admire you.'

He is laughing but he is rather sad too, he is rather sad and he will not come to the party, but he is glad that we asked him to come. So 'Good-bye, Aaron,' I call; and 'Good-bye, Pompey,' he says, 'Good-bye and good luck to you.'

I get my horse and ride down the street and at the corner I turn to look back. He is standing in the window upon the balcony. I wave good-bye, good-bye and ride on.

The party is already nearly over before I have realized that it is a very good party. If only, I think for a moment, lolling up against the bar to play with a piece of blancmange, coloured magenta, but blancmange for all that in its toute-entièreté of extreme boringness, if only darling Harriet were here, and my mind goes off to that Christmas dressing-up party in far away St. John's Wood, ah if only Harriet were here to see her Pompey lapping up magenta-mange, happy in this simple pleasure, but not again perhaps so simple, as blancmange à fourchette presents its own difficulties, by no means inconsiderable . . . when the party is *getting late* and the bottles (generously supplied in controversion of all Schloss Verbotens) empty. Ah, there is Haidée and her Baron. There is nothing remarkable about the Baron, I think, glancing above my poised mange-laden fork across the room at our Berlin friends, there is nothing about that boy to set the heartstream flowing upon a fancy's flight but the name which he has, that is this wonderful name, oh the most wonderful name, to set fancy a wing . . . upon a fool's errand. Aha. Festus Aurelian Baron von Borck. I set down my magenta entremet, I set it firmly down up the sideboard, and taking my half-full glass of gin and tonic I consider this Baron Festus Aurelian von Borck, interesting in nothing but an interesting name. And I drain my glass, turning again, in tearful disillusionment, for *what* a name, and heavens, might one not have expected, have hoped . . . ? But the man is a bore. I have just danced with him; and moreover, rather inclined as we are to be short of men, he has further complicated our unhappy situation by producing a gate-crashing sister of rather formidable aspect and an intensity of manner that is not at all a contribution to the party Gefühl that Josephine and I are doing our best to promote and maintain. I have been left alone with Fräulein von Borck earlier in the evening and for a period that was at once getting too long. Hurra, the last of magenta-mange has disappeared, tiptilting off my fork on to the floor, I regret to say, yes I am very sorry, but there it is, lying in a splodge at my feet. I toe it under the sideboard and hope that our excellent and silent staff will understand. But this Fräulein von Borck. Now for instance she will speak English and she will begin every sentence with

'Now look here.' Oh but that is a fault. 'Now look here. What do you pay for your accommodation in your London Wohnung', she has been saying that. I cannot no really I cannot be bothered to explain that I do not rent a Wohnung. That would lead to too many explanations involving my darling Aunt and would expose my extreme ignorance about our domestic budget, so I will give dear Harriet's rental instead. Oh but look here, says my Fräulein, Oh but look here, you cannot pay that, it is for instance impossible; you cannot pay so much, why for that in Berlin we could . . . (I forget what they could do in Berlin, rent the Eden may be.) Oh but look here, you cannot pay that. Well, as a matter of fact I don't, I think, and if Harriet likes to, that's no concern of yours, Gracious Miss. But then she will tell me about Germany, and that nobody can ever know, that nobody does know, that nobody *will* know (heart-thrust here at *ausländisches Ungnädigsein*) that nobody *will* know what Germany suffered in the 'twenties. Well it is not for want of telling. I am being so unsympathetic and so anxious to be off, this early moment of the party I am telling you. Like so many of her countrymen the Fräulein has the greatest, the most infantile admiration, for everything, but *everything*, englisch. But the englisch have hurt her very much, this poor Fräulein, oh very deep was the wound when the young Englishman, the son of a Bishop, oh that makes it so much worse, you see he was staying with the Fräulein to have his studies at the University, and what did he say one day but this, and was not this enough to divide the heart of a rhinoceros . . . 'England ought to conquer Germany and civilize her.' This boy, this son of the Bish, was very cross-patch indeed, I can see him chez Fräulein getting more and more cross-patch every day, till out he came with this heart piercing atrocity of a sentiment. Ah poor Germany, always to imagine what England is, and then to find out that is so much of what she is not. Oh this dotty infantile unsophistication of Deutschland, how exacerbating it is for grown-ups like England, France and America and how much of fuss-up it is making for Germany. It is like it was a cat foster-mothering a puppy that has got into her litter of young cats. 'Oh why will not his fur lie down? I lick, I lick. But up it goes again, (this imagination that Germany has of England). I lick, I lick, but up it goes again. It is absolutely heartrending.' Tears fill the eyes of the kind and dotty cat. 'Oh if only his fur would *lie down.*' England's (even at length to Germany obvious) declension from her dream-vision inspires at last a feeling not of sorrow but anger. It becomes a species of the basest treachery, a betrayal of an imagined blood brotherhood. Hence many tears and some flow of blood upon a hundred crazy battlefields. And hence, early in the party Pompey fugitive across the ball room to the safe anchorage and happy oblivion of the bar.

'And how is my little pig faring?'

It is Josephine. I begin to laugh, thinking of Fräulein von B. and the Bishop's son.

'Very full of magenta-mange and gin at the moment darling, and if ever you leave me near von Borck's sister again I'll wring your neck.'

'Have you see Lady Pym, darling Pompey, do just take a look at Lady Pym, she is confab with Miss Hatt at the moment.'

These are two of our old ladies, very dear friends they are, very lovey-dovey, very *intime* indeed. Lady Pym wears what Harriet always calls *English Lady's Cotton Dress*, but Miss Hatt wears attire of a more masculine cut. She always wears breeches in the daytime, which led to Colonel Peck's famous *mot*. It happened like this. I came into the smoking room one day and there was Miss Hatt standing astride the hearthrug, hands deep in the pockets of only *rather* well cut pants. So to open the conversation and make an excuse for siding her a pace or two up the mat, I said: 'Do you get much riding round here?' But that was not the right thing to say, oh indeed it was not. So later it was explained to me that Miss Hatt wore pants *on principle*. 'And a pretty fat principle too, if I may say so,' said Colonel Peck when I passed it up to him. Well this may not have sounded so-o-o funny at the time but remembered at a party that is *getting late*, and after a great deal too much Fräulein-and-gin, it sounds very very funny indeed. So Josephine and I started to laugh at it all over again. So after Josephine had had a drink we began to dance together. But you see Tom and the Colonel had deserted us, and the Baron was dancing with the Baronin, so what was there to do but dance with Josephine and have a good laugh. We pass Mrs. Pouncer sitting back in an armchair with her eyes closed and looking very docile and up to no tricks this time, but just any nice old lady having an old fashioned doze. And where are the spells and the enchantments, where have they flown away to now, dear Mrs. Witch? Tucked safely away in your nodding head, I have no doubt, and not flown away so far at all. Tom has come through the curtains and is standing in the doorway. 'Pompey,' he calls to me softly as we dance by. But I will not take any notice of him, I am listening to Josephine, she is telling me a very intriguing story about So-and-So. Mrs. Pouncer is asleep and dreaming. Perhaps she is dreaming happy old-lady dreams of far away England and kindly late husband, or perhaps she is dreaming lustier dreams of battle-scarred young men, waving enormous riding whips, and accompanied by their deliciously apprehensive female friends. Sleep on, kind Pouncer; whisper and grimace to your pleasure, dear Tom; I am for the moment free of you both, in a happy pause to laugh and scandalize with my dear Josephine.

The band plays faster, then faster faster play band, for we have the floor to ourselves and the walls are thronged with the tired white faces of the Schloss's invalids and captives; but we are not old and we are not tired but very happy and laughing and moving faster and faster together to the singing-singing swift-running notes of the musicians. Haidée and her Baron have withdrawn to stand by the long curtains of the window alcove, they are watching us very intently with a lick of a pure flame of a questioning surprise upon their pale faces. This is not *conforme*. Why surely this is not at all *conforme* that Josephine and Pompey should race together through the wide long room of the dance room of the Schloss with such a mad increasing pace, so swift, so swift with a something of a laughing abandonment that is not at all *conforme* but very peculiar indeed and rather shall we say a little incorrect in the thought that informs this quick running movement, why they are certainly running mad upon the dancing floor, why it is certainly the entire negation of correctitude. Oh Josephine and

I are suddenly so sick to death of old Schloss and its silent constraints, we are wishing so much to be wieder zurück in darling London in our darling parties to dance with our friends. But the hard bright white lights of the electric light chandeliers burn down upon us to thrust with disapproval and thrust down quietly quickly compellingly upon our moment of laughter and release. And our faces are a little pale now beneath these harsh lights, and there is a faint surge of an increasing fear to pull at our hearts and tap upon our dancing heels. But hurra, what do you think, at this moment that is beginning to be a little dangerous to our revolt, we have a reinforcement that we had not thought, a pair of allies, unexpected but twice welcome. Miss Hatt has pulled Lady Pym to her feet, and the grotesque friends are dancing together, dancing, dancing, to tread down with us the inimical harsh light that beats upon the ground, turning upward upon our dancing shoes. Brave old ladies, stalwart allies upon the turn of battle, Blücher himself was not more welcome.

Tom stands in the doorway, there is a great scowl upon his face, very cross indeed is this sweet Tom-boy, and he is saying something to himself. I wave to him, that makes him so furious, you know, he half steps on to the floor to pull me away, but I shall escape you Tom, my darling Josephine and

I will escape you and run quite away from all your commanding thoughts, your secret commands and insistences, so I laugh and laugh and wave, I am feeling so triumphant, you know, I am feeling. Oh it is to be so shot-up to be so completely free for a moment of compelling thought upon a Tom-thought, oh it is a great delight and pleasure for me, this moment, that has come suddenly with the sweet strength of the strong current of Josephine's thought, setting with mine upon the darling British Isles to meet in full stream, to grapple with and overcome the swift-running current of another thought that is set towards the east.

But the swift pure moment of elation and triumph is shrivelled and scorched to be burnt quite up and devoured by the flame of a touch upon my arm, a strong tearing movement with unthought-of strength that tears me apart from Josephine and swings me to the arms of too-ready Tom. It is the Pouncer that has suddenly woken from her old-lady dreams, that I think existed only in my frivolous party-imagination, it is the clutching tearing paw of this dainty Pouncer that has more strength in its delicacy than Tom could not have shown, that has this unholy witch-strength to tear apart and shatter entirely a bright swift thought that was so sweet to promise such a triumph of escape.

The Pouncer-witch, the insufferable sly old

widow, has taken Josephine away from me, leading her away from me across the room with compelling swift urgency that can only leave Josephine to turn her head a little for a good-bye that is unsaid. And the curtains swing behind me and the door closes upon my heels, and I am alone outside of the room with this ferocious young man. It is so sad you know, for me a little disappointing, and it is cold in the great hall, I am so cold, for I have no cape, my fur cape is inside the dancing room, and my dress is cut low to the waist at the back; it is so cold and so disappointing and severe, I begin to cry, I put my hands to my face, I begin to cry and nobody shall stop me. I cry and the tears fall between my fingers stretched to my face. Tom is so furious, so withdrawn and remote, he takes my arm to pull me across the hall and up the stairs, but I will not move, at least I will not move away from the door. So I am crying and the tears drip drip between my fingers to fall upon my dress.

But presently looking through my fingers I see that Tom's face has so much an expression of a violence hardly to be restrained for some remnant of good manners that it will almost come to the point of bursting; like he was so cross and so bottled up it is an impossibility for him to be more cross and more bottled up, but just too there is a little corner of a possibility that he will find out a way to become crosser, so that will lead the matter to a general conflagration an immense explosion which shall involve Pompey and the doorway and the whole of this reserved and sly Schloss Tilssen that has for many centuries I suspect, in a quiet way of its own mood, been up to no good, to not one good thing at all. So now I find the face of Tom very extremely amusing and I must begin to laugh instead of cry. But I think too, is this violent Tom to become a little tiresome with a tiresome masculine bully-dog mania that I could not tolerate, that would make me not cry or laugh but frowning in a hurried evasiveness turn away from him altogether? I do not like to be bullied at all, it is such a fuss-up and a noise, it is worse it is much worse than the Piccadilly underground railway in those sections of the line where they have not yet installed their shock-absorbers. So to avoid this very probable occurrence of bully-dog annoyance I run up the stairs in front of Tom and together we go into my room.

'Now Pompey,' says Tom, 'we must be off in half-an-hour. I'll run your bath for you and I'll give you ten minutes to have your bath and get into some clothes. I'll be back here by a quarter past.'

'A quarter past what?'

'A-quarter-past-twelve-what-do-you-think?' says Tom in a breath, a puff of furious violence. 'At a quarter past. Now mind.'

This very explicit Nanny-Tom prances off along the corridor to the bath room and I can hear the taps roaring in tune with his mood. Why do some women like to be bullied, I think to myself, lying at full length to enjoy the hot soft water. Now, at home where my aunt and I live, the wives are so often delighted to tell you how splendidly bullying their husbands are, and how they put the foot down here and there, and no, they will not let them play bridge in the afternoon and they will not let them smoke, 'My dear husband does not like to see me smoke', there is a great deal of pride in their voices when they say this, I have often noticed it, it is as if they would say, You may not think it but I am married to a tiger. No, I did not think it, for certainly I cannot penetrate this excellent disguise that this tiger has adopted, for certainly no better disguise for a tiger exists anywhere than the disguise of a Bottle Green husband. 'My dear,' say the jungle tiger-bucks, 'I shall go to the tiger reunion festival as a Bottle Green husband, you won't know me.'

I am back in my room now and slowly slowly I am dressing. My things are laid out for me across the bed, they are my riding clothes. I have now got to the stage of breeches shirt and boots and I am sitting on the bed to think. Tom comes in, he has got the waiter to bring up some hot strong coffee.

'Now for heaven's sake drink this and hurry up. Here's your coat and hat and gloves, and you'll want your riding mac.'

He puts my coat on me, buttoning it up to my chin almost, it is so tight and so constraining I feel that I am in a tight hard sentry box of a coat, but why it cannot be my coat, why my coat was never so tight as this coat is so tight, to hold me tightly, to press upon me and hold me in its tight harsh strength.

'Why Tom, my coat, this is not my coat.'

'Of course it's your coat, you fathead. Here take your gloves. I've got the mac.'

'But let me put my hat on properly, let me see that it is straight.'

'Don't go over to the mirror.'

Tom's voice has changed a little in tone, suddenly it is very quiet, not blustering or bully-dog at all, but very authoritatively quiet, as if it would not for one moment occur to this authoritative voice to be disobeyed.

'But I must see that my hat is on straight, and my hair . . .'

I go towards the long mirror across the room.

'Oh come along, there is no time.'

Tom switches the light off. But the fire is burning brightly in the fireplace and so I stand in front of the mirror with my hat in my hands to put it on my head in the correct manner. But oh how horrible how horrible is my reflection in the long mirror, and my hat stays quietly in my hands, I have no further thought for it at all. The flames on the hearth shoot up and their savage wild light is reflected at my collar, is held reflected and thrown back with a light that is more savage, but completely savage, with the flick of a savage quick laughter the light is tossed back again from the stars upon my collar and the buckle at my waist.

I am in uniform.

Oh how cold it is and rather damp too but so cold so bitterly cold. The wind is drawing from the east towards us as we ride, blowing the sleet-rain in our faces and the puffs of ground fog to drift upon our horses' fetlocks. I am riding my favourite horse, my darling prancing gay horse, that is called *Beau-Minon* and has something of that French elegance about him, to sit strangely upon an animal in these barbaric latitudes. He is a narrow polo pony and has the habit to turn suddenly contrariwise to the pull of the rein, which is the way that polo ponies have, and so you must be on your guard and think: Is that the rein I should pull, then it is the other I must pull, which makes you have to think about the horse and the riding when you would be off on your own thought-track to think of other things. But to-night Beau-Minon is a quiet sad horse picking his way severely and temperately with never a sideways glance or a thought to go setting him adance for the sake of a piece of white paper. Very sad he is, very contained and elegantly depressed. I am sorry for him, he has a long journey before, and behind, in the rain and against the wind, with something of the anxiety of the unknown, something that is a little threatening upon this wind that blows against us, to set the pine trees astir, to set them bending and lolling upon us against the steadfast wind that blows without ceasing. For many hours we have ridden through this wild night and now we are out upon the heath. We have left the pine woods far behind, it is a very blasted plain. The marsh pools reflect the stormy moonlight that is so wild and watery, to shine out one moment and light up the high night sky and the swift clouds rushing away to the west. Very deserted is this long stretch of marsh heathland, there is no house, no hut upon it, there is no road at all, we ride across open country. I keep close aheel of Tom, where he rides on to point the way for me.

We have not spoken one word all these many hours, we have ridden in silence. Is he still angry with me, or perhaps sad, and perhaps again a little –

well might he not be a little . . . to be feeling a little *involved* himself, that has involved me in this night adventuring towards the east, and always moving regularly and composedly towards the east, that is the east of our adventure? I am shy with Tom now, I feel very shy, for I like him so much, I like him very much indeed, and I do not wish to be a responsibility for him, and I do not wish to forget that I have promised to remember and remember and remember all the time, not as the fit takes me, but steadily to remember something that I have already forgotten and that was to be a help to him and to this Colonel Peck, who is already a little shadowy in my mind.

But this Colonel Peck, now wait, now just wait one little moment and remember to remember. For after that moment in my room at the Schloss, when first I saw myself in the long mirror in my bedroom to see and remark every point of light from buckle of belt and star-studded collar, after this moment, as we rode out of the gate of the Schloss, there stood this Colonel Peck to wave to us and wish us *bon voyage*, and as Tom rode past him he shook him by the hand and called up to him in the darkness, and the wind blew the words he said and brought them to me. And what did Colonel Peck say, it was about me, but it was nothing that you would have thought to hear him say such as: Take care, do not keep her too long in the saddle, no, it was nothing of this, what he said was: 'Look out she doesn't pinch your job.' And that makes me laugh now to remember this gay Colonel Peck and his warning words: 'Look out she doesn't pinch your job.' For wrapped as I am now in the long warm cloak that Tom has fastened round my shoulders, that he called in his deceitful moment 'your riding mac.' – my riding mac.! – It is *not* my riding mac., it is this long enfolding warm cloak that hangs straight from my shoulders and streams out behind me upon the rump of Beau-Minon, to keep him warm as well as me, and to be for a comfort to his cold cold rump.

And wrapped in this really magnificent and close, enfolding garment, this so-military apparel, I must laugh a little about this job-pinching business, to think of all that is stirring already in my heart; that this cloak is what there is for an outward and visible sign of my inward and spiritual sensation, growing growing with a strong swift growth to a full strength, that is what there is in my secret heart of pride and ambition, of tears and anger.

Oh how frightful are these sensations. Is not this all of all that I have ever experienced (and how often in these pages have they not informed my actions and my most secret motive) of this spiritual pride and intolerance, this anger like a flame upon the birth of all life, this turning towards darkness and death in darkness? Already there is a great joy in my heart to think that all is for ever over and passed away that had so much and so tediously to do with chère Josephine and Haidée, and the nagging mannerisms of the nagging, the overbearing, the so interfering *Schlossleben.*

So now I am free of all that, and of all that lay behind it, and of all that far-distant London life that, for an absence and freedom from a grievance and a self-injurious very great bitterness, I must seem not only to endure but to approve. 'I rejoice while I live in the tomb.' Hurra and hurra three times that this compulsory and commendable *rejoicing* is now for me for ever passed away. Let Titurel have his song of praise, his mimby-mamby reconciliation with his deplorable *status quo,* his bed-bottom false coming to terms with a life-in-death existence; for me no more, no more, no more ever again.

In my dreams I am always saying good-bye and
 riding away
Whither and why I know not nor do I care
And the parting is sweet and the parting over is
 sweetest
And sweetest of all is the night and the rushing
 air.

In my dreams they are always waving their hands
and saying good-bye
And they give me the stirrup cup and I smile as I
drink
I am glad the journey is set I am glad I am going
I am glad I am glad that my friends don't know what
I think.

When my darling Joey-parrot died . . . no I have told you that. But standing upright on his tail feathers to cry: What is come upon me? does not move me now or touch my withers, however wrung and wrung again are the Beau-Minon withers, to be set at late night upon such unfathomably motived departure. But I do not cry out for what is come upon me, I am indeed anxious not to know, in apprehension that it might prove to be something so ordinary, and in the ordinary way of ordinary journeying so set upon an ordinary *return*.

Ah my sweet Tom, you little guess that my silence, my unquestioning, is based upon a quick and too lively determination to resist all knowledge that might, however eventually, turn upon an explanation, and that again upon an *éclaircissement*, to enfold me, and upon an *ordinary* wing bear me back again to a life that is to me so profoundly so entirely unnecessary.

On on we ride, and thinking again these sad

thoughts I fall into tears, weeping silently for my *unnecessary* life; and pride, ambition, and all such light motives, are drowned a hundred times deeper than the loftiest mountain peak in the flood of a thought upon death. But since I am thus desperately out of love with life, in war shall I not do well, so well as my Pouncer has wished me, so well so very well? For the gods laugh very much when people go to war to be done with life, they laugh very much and turn aside the swift glancing weapons of Death, that are for happy people only, and for hearts that are not reconciled to him. Indeed this is the best joke the gods have, and they are like a child in the boring way they will have their joke, and have it to play it out again and again, with never a yawn for tedious repetition. 'Fear and be slain they only may . . .'

But fear not, snap your fingers in the face of death in his most frightful aspect, it does not matter, hunt him down, he will evade you. So this is rather a pity and sets my thought upon a major disillusionment. I guess I am not now purposed for death at all but for a high-up commission and a staff hat. And perhaps they had been talking about me, and perhaps I had, in all my days at the Schloss, rather unconsciously given myself away, so that talking about me they had come to this conclusion about me, that there was in me this rather dangerous desperation that might be used or that might – horrible thought – use them, and this conclusion of the gossiping two soldiers itself informed the last words of Colonel Peck: 'Look out she doesn't pinch your job.'

But I guess too there is much work to be done when at some distance in time and space we shall have arrived. And this thought is not distasteful to me, for I am heavy with a knowledge that is not my knowledge, and almost with the experience of a military strategy that certainly is not my own. But this knowledge and this experience is so shadowy it does not at all press upon my consciousness, to cause me anxiety or dismay, or a sense of strain for a talent that is to be at last tried out, and put to the stress of test and proof upon a critical occasion. There never was anyone than I less full of apprehension; on this familiar count. And if the knowledge and the experience are not wholly mine, neither I suppose is the confidence that waits upon them. But only at this moment a very present and actual sensation of cold, stiffness, tiredness (and all of those incidentals of campaigning upon a blasted heath beneath inclement weather) is paramount. And a village Hampden, a Cockney strategist, may have their moments of humanity – a sniff a whine a tear, a lost handkerchief.

Oh poor poor Beau-Minon, is this blasted ride to have no end? Tom has broken into a canter to take a wide-spread ditch some yards ahead. But can

Beau-Minon *do it*? Is it not perhaps rather to ask the cruelly unreasonable, at this time of early morning, after this long and so-exhausting ride? I touch him with my heel. But oh, I am so cold, and the stirrup steel burns icily beneath my foot. Oh come on, come on, Beau-Minon, this is not a time to check and be so cross, to check and prance, to dance sideways and to dissipate in this absurd antic so much of your energy and of mine. Now come on, my dear Beau-Minon, for if you toss me into that ditch it will be the death of a cold for me, and a death that I am not at all hankering after, to lie and suffocate with a cold in the head, and a something in the bronchial passages to make an end of all night-riding. Beau-Minon responds, breaks into a canter, skims the ditch, lands, pecks at the landing, and shoots me over his head on to the beastly damp soft marsh slime. Tom has deigned to turn his head, he comes back, props me on to my unsteady frozen feet and sets me in the saddle again.

'Do *try* and stay on, Pompey,' he says; he is still and after all these hours it is to me surprising that he can still be so cross. 'Do try and stay on.'

'Hurra Tom, you have spoken.' It is as if I had caught him out at some game, and I have won.

'Do *try* and stay on, we are over the frontier now. That ditch was the frontier.'

'And is there any reason why I should more

necessarily stay on *over* the frontier than *not* over the frontier? And did we have to come all this way to see a ditch with a tricky landing on the other side, and did we? And do you suppose I fell off, do you suppose I fell off for my own advantage? And do you not suppose that I am very uncomfortably cold and tired? And Tom, let me add this, are we never going to get anywhere, are we never going to get anywhere that is not a blasted heath, an exposed place, a draught and a burden?'

'We sleep by day and ride by night.'

'And if there is no moon shining, that will be difficult, dangerous to our horses and ourselves, and on the last count unnecessary.' For never did I see a less inhabited landscape, or less habitable, or a less pleasing prospect, or a more noticeable absence of the vileness of mankind.

But thank heaven the day is now breaking and the wind-swept watery and abandoned sky is streaked with a little, a very little grey streak of a daybreak over against the dark horizon of this sodden plain.

There is rather an unpleasant subnatural feeling about this country. It looks so lost, so utterly forlorn, so woebegone so Come-what-may-I-do-not-care, so very desperately resigned upon a weight of memory. And every stunted naked tree and bush, and every blade of thinnest palest grass, is straining away, and streaming away – that cannot stir but longs to be away, that is straining and turning and pointing towards the ditch of demarcation, to be across the other side and away, that cannot stir. I have the feeling that we are moving steadily in the wrong direction, but it is at the same time a necessary direction, a dangerous direction. We had better look out.

Later on we have come to our rest house. And a very low squat disagreeable looking house it is, but the day is fully upon us now and we must be glad of shelter. There is an old crone that brings us food and hot water. Well I take my share of the hot water first, and when I have had a nice hot wash, (taking off my belted and bestarred coat and shirt to make a good wash) I am feeling better though real unearthly tired. Then Tom has his nice hot wash, and it is still rather cold in this extremely dark house, with only thin barred slits for windows. So we breakfast fully dressed and buttoned up again in our hateful uniforms, with our elegant lovely travel-cloaks across the chairs behind us.

Tom is become more genial. We laugh a good deal at breakfast and get quite exicted.

'Oh Tom, only you should not have put me into this coat, yes Tom, indeed you should not. I do not like to be in uniform, to prance round and be a soldierly female, I have a sort of horror of that sort of female, that is always bouncing about and being so uniformly and so controllingly upstage and arbitrary, it does not sit well with the female, I do not like it. And oh Tom, (I run to him at once again, rather serious) Is it necessary? Why must I wear this coat that is already putting such unfemale thoughts into my head?'

'Oh it is, is it?' says Tom, laughing and dandling a tepid potato upon his fork. 'Glad to hear it. What with all the snivelling and whining, the sobs and tears, lost stirrups and final cropper I began to wonder . . .'

'Oh Tom,' I cry again, in a last desperate shift of seriousness that is already running to laughter, 'we shall each outdo each in cruelty. Oh this coat. Oh it is so detestable. And the thoughts that go with it, they are so utterly detestable.'

'Any more of that Pompey, and I'll wring your neck, Pompey die Grosse or no Pompey die Grosse.'

Pompey die Grosse. Pompey *der* Grosse. Der Tod Pompeys des Grossen. The savagery and success of *that* war runs up sudden upon my memory, and I have a picture of the low uneven hills, and the long straight road black with legionaries, and the low uneven hills, with so many crosses, so many crosses against the evening sky, and upon each cross . . . Oh no, No, no. I hide my face in my hands not to see the crucified, and the white pebbles glancing from the hand of the young emperor, that is another picture upon a picture.

I stand up and begin to unbutton my coat, to take off my uniform, to sleep. Tom comes to me now and lifts me up in his arms. I am really sleepy now, so deliciously sleepy, so heavy with this delicious sleepy drowse. Tom holds me up in his arms, lets me slip for a moment and hoists me again, and from high up in his arms I smile down upon him. No really, it is impossible, I am so tired, so pleasantly tired, in the thought that I shall soon be asleep. I don't care for the crucified really you know, some people are born that way, some people are born to be crucified, and was it not in this instance an old Roman custom, that was only perhaps rather a *waste of time*, in a way that might have appealed to the practical Romans, to make an end of it, and another sort of end of *them*? I laugh and laugh with delight, and smile down into the eyes of Tom, dear Tom, and thank the God of War to be rid of the tea-cups and tattle and the boring old do-all-nothings of a finished existence.

He holds me high in his arms, the room is very dark, very low ceilinged, it is a long dark low room, the day has come, but it is a dark cold day, rather hopeless and set in in a grey half light upon itself, very close-kept you would say is the secret of this sad quiet daylight that blows up upon the windy sky from the east, I can see it through the high window, I look through the high window, held high in his arms, I look through and from a great height down and across the window-framed picture of the vanishing flat rainsodden plain that stretches far away with never a sign of habitation but ours and never a tree or a bush or a blade of grass that is not bent and twisted beneath the blowing high wind. There is no sound of gunfire, there is no sound at all; in spite of the thin driving rain there is a little ground fog too, does the ground fog muffle the sounds of war, the echo of the heavy gunfire I have heard before, sitting above the cliffs at Tilssen, or is there no sound of war but the thought, only the thought in suspension of the sound of a regular firing from masked and heavy artillery?

It is curious that this side of the frontier and now by so many miles there is so little of the actuality of war, but only to be had in remembrance now and again the thought of it, and on the other side of the frontier there was so much of the war materialismus that was actual, the clever arrangement of the money, the draft upon New York, the tragic fatality of the thoughts of dear Aaronsen, the long morning rides with Tom, riding up and through the woods and out at last upon the clearing before the fortress, and mounted high upon that fortress the old old guns and the name upon them, again it comes to my mind, this name that is a very actual warlike password 'Birdie, Birdie, Strand and Dolland', with what of a linking up with the cities of London and New York and the secret swift dark current of finance bearing upon it the curd and foam of the very essence of the movement of armies.

But here all is quiet and deeply quiet and silent, and cold so cold, with only the fog and the rain and the grey sad day to look out upon. Tom moves his arms, he shifts his position to shake me a little, I look down to smile at him again, all of my weight is upon his arms, and his face is raised to mine. This is a curious and amusing inversion, this smiling smiling upturned Tom-face and my weight pressing down upon the lifted arms, I am held high up in the cold dark room high up into the darkness of the dark ceiling above the narrow slit window-panes that are barred across and across. Why there is almost something of a fortress in this abode of draughts and discomfort. Oh let me down, let me down, Tom, or I shall become into a frozen remoteness to be for ever spreadeagled against the cold darkness of the dark ceiling.

Night comes and we are in the saddle again. And so it is for many days and nights. Always with the dawn we are come to a rest house that is dark and cold and draughty, and always there is an old man or an old woman to bring us something that is looking like Irish Stew in a great pot with enormous great soup plates into which the lumps of hateful fat meat and turnips are ladled, and eat we must and eat we must or go hungry. Oh how horrible it is, Oh Tom how deeply bored I am with these dark rest houses, these cold prisons for our day-times, these prisoners' ladlings of disgusting fat meat and abominable turnips that have caught to the side of the pan a little, yes always they are tasting a little burnt, you know, well suppose, it is not very pleasant for us. But Tom is only amused to laugh a little and so we come to getting together accustomed to the discomforts until we come to arriving. Now there have been some people we have passed riding, since we are arriving, not now so cautiously by night time, but in the open daylight, and we have passed (it is rather foggy) we have passed bands of men. Poor men, they look very trampish, their faces are so tired and quite blank, and they move their heavy feet, and do not look at us as we pass upon our grand horses, wrapped closely in our cloaks.

These are friends of ours, yes? They are wearing our uniform, this beastly green fungus-coloured dun grey uniform, but their buttons are tarnished and they have no buckles at their belts to throw back any reflections of a bright white hot light, fire burning bright heat of any light at all, they move leaning their heavy bodies forwards, they move away from us into the mist, and into the mist of the great boles of the forest trees, for again we are again in thickly wooded country, where there is cover for all, cover for all.

The sound of the feet of the tired men stumbling through the forests and cracking the thick undergrowth is again the only sound we can hear, all else in these sad regions is silent, with a hopelessness of a silence that has given up the thought of speaking or crying out aloud at night time. And for why? Because it is no use, no use at all. Silence there is, and a quiet sadness, and an immense great silence of sadness, leading to an ultimate slow numbness of the spirit, in a little death.

I harden my heart against this little death that numbs the spirit and leaves only the feet to move in a heavy rhythm, in an accustomed slow path of a physical mechanism, I harden my heart indeed against these poor men, that are our men, and am come to think of them as a bore, because they are moving I guess in the wrong path. But we shall have something to say about that, yes, we shall have something to say, and there will be something that we can do, that Casmilus in association with Satterthwaite will for certain bring to pass.

Oh hurra. Now this is more comfortable, but this is absolutely fine, you know it is very grand and slap-up this last and final abode of ours, it is a very great improvement upon the rest houses that we have had upon our way, and we are treated with great deference as becomes becloaked commanders, and the men, the automatons upon their tired feet, walking numbly upon a little death, are ours, to move this way and that, to command and to visit with rewards and penalties.

But the war and the actuality of this evasive war, and the actuality of the tired tired men, drifts away from us again, shut up in our high tower girdled by a swift deep river and looking down upon a wide sweep of lofty forest trees, with here and there in the distance broad lakewater, with reeds to fringe its margins, and within the reeds the wild duck we go to shoot by daytime, in a flat-bottomed boat, that is at the same time a diversion for us and a practice for me to have with my gun.

But I am getting better with my gun. Already I am so much better than I was when I was out shooting in dear England, over the shoot in Essex, where, with Ian Crawford and his friend Guy for my companions, upon a Sunday, and with little care for the severe gaming laws, we shot pheasant and duck, blazing away into the coveys that rose to our dog's barking against the evening-bright sky.

Oh I do love going shooting with you and Guy, oh it is delightful to go round the fields on Sunday evening, oh how I do like to do this.

Oh yes, Pompey, (Ian is saying this) Oh yes, Pompey, and your idea of going round the fields to shoot on a Sunday evening, is to go round the fields a couple of yards behind me and keep up an endless flow of conversation with Guy, that is enough to put a hare on its guard three fields away.

But Guy likes to talk, Ian, it isn't me so much as for Guy's sake that we talk. If it was not for Guy I should walk in absolute and complete silence, you would not know I was there, I assure you that you would not.

But Ian was wanting me to bite through the neck of the pheasant he did not quite succeed in killing.

But I have had toothache all the weekend and now it is better and now I am certainly not going to take the risk that it will come back again, to bite through the neck of your only indifferently shot pheasant. And if for instance you want your pheasant to be absolutely and entirely dead, you should aim a little ahead, and place your shot with more skill, but that is only something rather unfortunate for you, for I know that for most times you are a good shot, but it was perhaps just this once. – Very well then, knock the head of the pheasant upon the ground, but do not expect for one moment that I will take it in my teeth to bite through its neck.

Now this makes me laugh to remember this, that all the time I have been walking with Ian and Guy, I have been carrying my little ·20 bore shotgun, and it is loaded, and we have crawled through ditches and through hedges, and so when we come back at last to the old farmhouse in this wide open delightful Essex country, as we are coming through the garden to come up to the house, Guy says to me:

'Pompey, I always remember the first thing my father taught me when as a boy I first went shooting with him was: "Always unload before you crawl through a hedge, my boy," he said, "always unload for there are more shooting accidents come that way than you would ever believe possible, so remember to unload, it is boring perhaps, but not so boring as to have a shot of lead into your side".'

But this Guy was a very peculiar man, very peculiar in his head, that had this sort of time-lag in his thoughts, to go to warning me so solemn and so late upon the event. But it was shellshock in a peculiar way that he was suffering from, having suffered very much in the last war and become apt in this way to talk too much when he was shooting and to warn me instead of before, after.

But there was something sweet about Guy, and

very much I liked and admired him for the way that he was able to build up his life and to enjoy it so much in spite of this confusion he had about the passage of time, and an almost Einstein *pratique* in his regard for its past and future tenses.

So I was often thinking of all this when out with my immediate shooting and fascinating duck-shooting companion, this dear Tom that was also my war crony and fellow campaigner.

Oh how very beautiful this was, to go out with him upon the reedy lakes, to hunt the wild duck, to come back tired at night to a steaming jugful of hot water that is poured into a zinc bath set upon a pile of blankets that is laid upon the floor.

But after dinner every night we do a lot of hard work that is a peculiar great pleasure to me.

We have our secret telephone that connects to the heart of Headquarters, many miles away, we do not know where it is, not yet.

But always the messages are coming through, they come through in halves, so very cautious is this pan-jandrum of a Chief of Staff, so that we must copy them down as they come in the childish sweet voice over the telephone, in the childish language that is a superlatively grand code for which Tom must ask my help. And then the second half will come through, and we sit down, and by the light of a candle, to call less attention to us, by the light of this candle illuminating the whitewashed brick walls of the room where we work, we sit down to fix the messages together and to get the heart of the sense out of them.

But I am so fascinated by this grand code-game and by the correlation of these separate messages that go to make so much of nonsense, and only after long hours of concentration and bewilderment at last a sense that is so clear it is almost a blow between the eyes. And always it is to do with the swing and pulse of the movements of the troops of the armies, and the shifting flickering prize that is not yet for the one or the other.

Ah how fascinating to me are these night watches. With the shade pulled over my eyes I work and work and it is a pleasure to me, a peculiar great pleasure so that Tom must make up a rhyme about it to laugh and say:

O quid solutis est beatius curis
Nothing at this time Pompeia's quite sure is
More beneficial delightful and kind
Than the sweat of the brow to an overwrought mind.

But I am so happy in this work, it is a great pleasure to me, it is to forget the endless tiresomeness of a usual existence, oh may it never come again. I am so happy as I have never been, with a tranquil happiness that waits in patience upon a future event, that is not quiet, or perhaps so happy, and is not yet.

The frost has come now, the ice and the snow. And with the outbreak of winter there is a quickening in the tempo of our lives. Outside of our tower by daytime there is white and gold and winter blue. How much worse it is now for the fighting men. The slightly wounded will lie by night on the cold battlefields to die from exposure in the bitter dark night. And often now I am out at night, for there is disaffection upon the air and the war is drifting our way.

And I am in fine fettle, not tired at all, or any longer set to a mood of obstinate abstraction, to grumble at the food, to send back to the kitchen the disgusting fat meat, the tepid coffee, to be so icily furious because of the draughts in our tower house, to come out of this mood at some times only, with a great enthusiasm for the telephone, this mysterious telephone that only has the power to hold me, in complete concentration, in a swift ambitious elation, as the voice comes through upon the secret wire – the peculiar soft voice.

Very soft and winning is the voice of the unseen

speaker, with a lisp here and there and a soft quick laugh to point the rhythm of the quite horrifying quick short sentences that come to me, sitting at my telephone table, to listen and listen and take fire of pride at a sudden swift comprehension of a word, a sentence, that should not have been understood.

But now this question of food, this is not so lightly to be shelved, by whatever of a change in our northern climate, by whatever pressure of a growing sensation in myself of a physical wellbeing, ambition, pride and a little of intolerance.

Well for instance, hardened and stoicized as I am in a desperation of an eat-or-go-hungry ultimatum, as I am and must be after so many years of London restaurants, it is something, is it not, that I am exasperated beyond endurance by the food we must eat on this side of the frontier, that I am driven so to complain in a diurnal reiteration of a general fuss-up and perpetual internecine warfare with our abominable commissariat.

I guess the hardening process of dear Tom's upbringing must in its character have been something almost not to be thought of so far in excess of the barbarity of a mere *London* eating house, that he can even now munch and swallow, without a murmur or a growl or the elevation of an eyebrow, the burnt porridge, the abominable coffee, the viscous and tepid olla podrida of a cook's imagination, so evil in its essence, so abandoned and unprincipled, uninformed by the merest whisper of a mere question of humanity.

So for myself, now looking back upon my Piccadilly lunches of many fresh and hopeful departures, I must imagine myself to have been something over-fastidious, and the restaurant of no mean skill with pot gridiron and frypan.

Ah these London houses of refreshment, how they also bring back to me the image of my dearest Harriet, who has too long been absent from my thoughts, and the incidence of our adventuring together in and out and around of that half mile or so within pointing distance of Eros and his arrows.

With a swift visualization as of something clearly focussed in an otherwise blurred film sequence, I can see again the little cake-shop-cum-restaurant where so often we have lunched together, lunched that is to say, if one may use the word for so slight a choice, upon a sandwich and a pot of English Lady's luncheon coffee.

There was something that happened one day at this restaurant that made Harriet and me laugh that I will now tell you. Now this restaurant it was mostly patronized by rich old ladies that you would have thought to have some arrogance in the handling of a domestic situation. But no it did not work out quite like that at all, for the arrogance was all upon the side of the waitress that for haughtiness pride and caprice I have not met the like of.

And the old rich old ladies, lined up upon a long series of padded sofas behind tables too closely neighboured, of the wrong height, shape and constitution (so weak, so cheap, so uneven of leg and surface), must wait and sing and whistle and bang upon the caprice of the waitress that would, and would not come, that disappeared behind staff doors letting upon a chaos of badtempered cracking of dishes, slapping of dish-rags and the uneasy sound of a knife upon steel, to issue again, Demeter-like, and descend upon her votaries, to appear on this occasion, select her favourite, and cry in Nanny-like tones of No-nonsense-from-you-Miss, 'Ready for your figs?'

Gulping and choking in our coffee cups to conceal for cowardice a desperate mirth, Harriet and I survey the scene, mark the light of hope kindling in eye of fig-fan, and the superb and sudden arrogance of *her* deportment, thus favoured, thus selected . . . Non sum digna.

But this dear picture, with the sounds the sight the smell the very essence of that substantial triviality of a daily experience, has faded from my leica-memory, and I sit here within my tower beside my desk, I sit on into the dark night, so cold I am now, so silent, wrapped in upon a security of separation from this London memory, that was at the time not thought of for one moment to be remembered and laid aside, to let lapse again upon another thought.

Ah the fascination of this telephone. The lisping, the laughter, the almost, well was it? – a giggle, the sweetness of the high lisping sweet singing voice that comes to my ears upon my secret wire. And these simple words, so childlike in their simplicity, so horrifying in significance, are to be recorded for ever it seems, burnt in upon a memory that was too feeble. But is not, is not now.

The movements of armies, the death of men, how many days have passed? The tactical experiment upon a tilt of death, the massing of reinforcements, the approach of . . .? Well, what is it?

'Something definite at last, thank God,' cries Tom above my shoulder.

'We lost very heavily at Mentz, Tom. The Archbishop is not very pleased.'

'It was a risk we had to take.'

'I don't agree.'

I take my cloak, pull on my furred helmet and long fur gloves.

Was there ever anything so dark as this dark night, so dark, so cold, so deathlike in its silence, so venomous in secrecy? Use my torch I dare not, for I am not less venomous and secret than the night. But later, with the dim light of our tower room far behind me, in memory by contrast brilliant, I become accustomed to the darkness and can pick my way upon the hard surface of frozen snow. Looking up between the tufted branches of the trees I can see the stars. There is no moon.

Starlight has always had an effect of the uneasy upon my mind, so cold, so distant, unfreundlich, so remote. It disturbs and excites me, calling to everything that is in me of the inhuman, the disembodied, the separate. It also makes me feel to be pitted against a most inhuman enemy, with an answering swift increasing power in my veins, a desperate defiance, to lift my arms and cry in something of a barnstorming vehemence Feindliches Licht!

Why is it starlight so disturbs our kind
Dissipates the purposes of the human mind
Empties familiar things of all significance
And sets the thoughts in an inconsequent dance
Making the loftiest and ruling of them sit mumchance?

It is so cold. I am out of the wood now and across the plain where the bitter night wind blows unhindered so that I must bury my face in my furlined cloak, my arm bent up beneath it for a shield.

I have some miles to go, making use as I can of what cover I find, there is little enough.

There is no doubt about it, no doubt at all, that our losses were too great, and Tom's judgment at fault. Tom has a certain obstinacy, an assurance of long years of professional soldiering. But lately he has become . . . I do not know, it is a little thought that has been growing upon me, I do not know. But I have succeeded where he has failed, and the messages that come through to us are for me and not for him.

No longer do we have our laughing quick happy days and nights together, no longer am I to be cajoled, informed, delighted.

How happy those days were, too happy, they could not last.

Likely when put to the test, was *their* expectation of me. But the long happy days of winning me over from a quite excessive inattention are passed away. Have they not by this time become almost too successful, what am I now, and set to what?

There is a despondency in my heart, no, it is an absolute darkness of ferocity about and within me, it is partly to think that these happy days are swung again to their close, and the rhythm of separation and ferocity succeeds.

And I that used to cry so easily, so quickly laughing and so quickly again in a human sadness of swift tears, so apt for human comfort and the happiness of a shared experience, have no tears now, am shut in upon myself, have no tears, no sadness and no joy.

But only in my heart a something that is hardly to be borne, so completely arrived, so appalling in its promise of a swift growth, so dark in its ferocity.

And as I grow stronger Tom grows weaker, on occasion petulant, frivolous, irrational and obstinate.

And he becomes a frowning babe
And all is done as I have said.

How arbitrary is the rhythm of existence, with mood succeeding mood and power shifting from hand to hand.

In the morning yesterday, riding through the village, there was a demonstration against us, and stones flung at me, not at him. And there was something almost to laugh at in the immense chagrin of this once so dear Tom, that it was Pompey got the dirty looks, the stone flung wide of her conceited head. I laugh now, but it is not a very friendly laugh, and there is still something in me to be appalled at its hateful undertone.

I have done my work for this night. I have crept up to the lighted window, have looked up and found my point of vantage. Climbing with some difficulty (these heavy clothes are not best suited to it), I have stood upon the balcony against the window. I can only *see*. There are four men inside of the room. Well that is something to know, I did not suppose voices would penetrate the double-paned fast-closed windows.

It is a little dangerous perhaps to climb down again and in at an opened lavatory window, but I have done this because it is also rather exciting, you know, a thing I have done before sometimes, it is rather a good joke, and so nice for a change to be inside-of, instead of perpetually and draughtily outside-of, whatever the not-to-be-imagined possibilities of discovery and happenings upon it. So eventually, with my lucky star ascendant on a too favoured course, I can hear what is said, and can come off safely with a suspicion I have had confirmed.

We have got something in pickle for these conspirators, but not for a week or two, and it is something that dear Tom knows nothing about, but only I do, and only I in close night-talk with Generalissimo Clever-Pie at Headquarters, with this lisping diabolic child voice that has promised me, Not So-and-So but So-and-So (naming a swift and most irregular promotion) dear Pompey, *if you succeed.*

These four men inside of this room are such absolute fools, such complete little sillies, so devoted to a dotty idea, and so kindly involving in their dottiness so many, so temptingly many of an unarmed enemy.

Well that is getting rather funny-ha-ha, do you know, with something of a funny situation to come to pass and a little bloodshed? . . . well, it is a pity for them, it is a great pity they did not think to keep it to themselves. And yet is it such a pity?

I think the Archbishop will be pleased, it will make up to him a little for Tom's stupid, and to his Eminence naturally disturbing, loss of life upon a fruitless tactic that should never have been made. *Thou shalt do no murder*, but if you must, let it be the enemy and not our own wretched troops, poor material as they are and so hardly to be frightened and cajoled into enlistment.

Thinking about this, and laughing a little to myself, I take a short cut across a vegetable patch and straddling the high stockade to make an escape to open country I find myself held by the leg. By God what is this? Will the bunny-fur of Tom's once sweet concern fly now? Not if I can help it. I look down from my precarious perch. The high wind still blows from the north, and the stockade is inconveniently arock. Some unwise human hand has hold upon my riding boot. I flash my torch, since I am caught it is no matter, into a face that is so rat-like, so wizened, so remote from all accepted standards of a dignified old age, that I am a little held and interested.

Very yellow is this face, allowing for the yellowing effect of torchlight, very yellow, with the skin sweat-beaded, pulled tight across cheekbone and bald scalp. Above me is the wide open high night-sky, below me the little yellow face of this – monster of rat-faced eld. For monster it is, as I peer closely and at leisure (no offence, no offence, my dear sir, and – no hurry) into his eyes, I am enchanted by the meanness of a crafty cruelty and malice that I see there. The paw upon my boot tightens its grip and turns slightly to wrench the bone in its socket. No matter, the boot will stand that treatment, and my knee is securely tight against the fence in a grip firmer than ever Beau-Minon knew. My eye travels over his face, the flat nose, the nostrils splayed and broken at the edges, the saliva dripping from too slackly open lips, the teeth, long, yellow, filthy, like dog's fangs upon the edge of a really shockingly illkept moustache. Cruelty, hostility, obstruction, how often have I not seen the reflection of this unamiable character upon a human countenance. Cruelty, hostility, obstruction, upon no dotty ideal, upon nothing so in contrast reputable, upon a smugness rather, upon a smug insufferable conviction; the backside of the world; the smug flat note of *that* vox humana, *We are so many*.

Yes, I have seen it before, this rat face; in London, Berlin, Paris, New York; in the villages of Hertfordshire. And now here, in this ultima Thule of beyond the frontier, and now here? *We are so many:* You shall be so many, less one. And to my liberalistic world-conscience, that is still persisting in Opposition, I may say: He must not live to tell the tale, to put a something in jeopardy that must be secure.

I draw my revolver. Now, dear Reader, do not imagine that this is a flourishing grand gesture upon a fence at midnight. On the stage, at the cinema, it might be so. A splendid ridiculous sweep, up and down, quick-pat fire, and away upon the echo of a shot. But not so when it comes upon the left hand, upon a fence arock in a high wind, upon a precarious knee-and hand balance, with a booted leg held and twisted, to make the bone grate a little in its socket, with an ominous thought for a sprained knee-cap, set awry and dislocated, with attendant penalties of lameness and enforced reliance upon an unkind host.

My revolver, I have it free at last, with a clumsy fumbling you may picture for yourself. I have the thought to put the barrel between the long yellow dirty teeth, that open so invitingly upon slack lips. How disagreeable he looks, I think he must soon be dead, yes, I think he cannot live very long, why look, how old and cold he is, with underneath the yellow a creeping tide of a cold grey flood upon cheeks and brow. Yes, I think in any case he must be dead soon.

Tom is sick now. We have had him sick for many days. I am so sorry for Tom. But my thoughts cannot stay with him, I must leave orders with the servants, and always I am having to go out, riding swiftly upon Beau-Minon, that has recovered her former good spirits, that is again my darling Beau-Minon, so fleet and sure of foot, so pleased and proud, shod in roughed shoes for this tricky going upon hard slippery paths.

'There is so much to do, you see, dear Tom, I cannot stay.'

And then he will say: 'Take the receiver off, let them rip. What concern is it of ours any longer? Take the receiver off, cut the line, let them rip and rot. It is winter now, we have been here too long, there are no letters, no mail from Tilssen, we must go back.'

And then he will say: 'Pompey, Pompey, what are you doing?'

'Why, Tom, I am sitting at the table, just sitting to write my telegrams, I am here my dear, but do not call me so often.'

'You are busy?'

'Why yes, Tom, there is a lot to do, you know, there is so much to do.'

'And Generalissimo Clever-Pie, he is pleased, eh? And the Archbishop? He is very pleased I suppose?'

'Why yes, Tom, they are pleased.'

I do not tell him that it has been a great success, the idea I had, that was crystallized the night I shot Rat-face, Rat-face that had something so fleeting-familiar upon his beetle eye, something that did not at all belong to the essence of the heart of Rat-face, that was flashed upon his eyes by a thought, it must have been my own, from some far place of a dark memory, to rise up with an impertinent incongruity, an altogether out-of-character impertinence; to rise up, to question, to question my commission, with a surge-back to a voice that never spoke, but in a dream of weakness: *From whom do you hold your commission?* Away, ghost of nightmare, begot by fear upon calamity. From whom do I hold my commission? I shall know very soon. For I am ordered to Mentz, to see the Archbishop.

Dear Tom, what a sweetie-pie he looks, tucked up to the chin, beneath a white bear-skin; rather sick, but getting better.

Outside of our room is the cold frozen cold dark night fields, and upon them the war that goes backwards and forwards, and the fighting men by daytime give their scarlet blood to the white snow and the golden sunshine.

Oh how evil is the heart of men and the scarlet of its blood that is so ready to be outpoured upon so ignoble an occasion. For pride and revenge the blood flows out, and for a foolish ideology that I saw writ up so plainly to flicker upon the inspired wooden faces of the soldiers I had shot down.

Oh flickering like a flame upon each face, raked by my field glasses, how frightful it was, and how amusing to be able to destroy.

And was this for cruelty that the scarlet blood flowed, flowing out upon the ground in a stream to carry with it and away all of that dotty idealismus, that was but a deceit of the black devil, that will have us all to destroy us, to bring us to destruction, if he can he will do this. We must be wary to avoid the occasion.

But is not the devil also in the hands of the destroyer, that shoots and slays, to destroy, to make an end, that can make no end, that only God can make?

And on this snow-white dark night, with Christmas upon the air, lying beneath the white bearskin rug upon the low bed to look at Tom, I am wondering if ever these heartrending and ferocious thoughts within my own head were ever for a moment within his, and if my success, with what outcome it may have, is not due to this fury and desperation, and white bright light of hatred for the evil of cruelty, to brood upon it, to magnify and relate, with the swift-running, ever counter-running current of our human thought, that has in it so much of a fatality, so much a cause for tears.

But Christmas is upon the air again, and the celebration of the birth of Christ draws near, and how must our thoughts not turn to Him when all men turn against us, and in this false approach find what? — our own best thoughts, be-haloed and enthroned, the apotheosis of *our* preference. Yes, no, yes, no, of course we must think of Christ at a moment like this, and take the rags of an old theology between our teeth. Better to give the baby a bone ring than the infected dummy of that thought. Ah Christ, *that* Christ, more wronged, tormented and again crucified within the minds of men since his death upon the cross, than ever in his lifetime by what simple misunderstanding of Jew and Roman; in history betrayed, in philosophy dislimned, how come to an end, how make an end at all in the silence of the grave, that is not for a certain nescience, oh not this at all?

If my thoughts with the impetus of centuries must turn and run upon theology, let them make a halt at Genesis and consider the Almighty, a gusty Creator in the manner of Rubens, and laugh out loud with Behemoth and Leviathan and say: Three cheers for the animals of the first week. Oh yes, oh yes.

How profoundly evil are our thoughts, and set upon a wilderness of lies, how come to an escape, how be free of our inventions, and the devil that is so skilful to be always within them? Yes, yes. Inside of the array of our most highest thoughts and seeming pure desires is his best good.

In England there is no national ideology, or not one that is formed, to be carried through, to be expressed in a word and impressed upon a people, as in Germany it is expressed and impressed, with what of an original pure intention we cannot know, with what of a calamity in event we know too well.

And upon this side of the frontier it marches with the enemy, it informs their dotty heroism. But we shall win, we shall win. We have the arms and the money, the mercenaries and the riff-raff of many armies. Death to the dotty idealismus, death to all ideologies; death upon the flying bullet that has been paid for; death from the bent form of the hired soldier; death upon the wind from the north.

And we are right, we are right; however riff-raff our armies, however base our honey-voiced Headquarters, known but to this point by me upon the telephone wires, to be known shortly in person at Mentz, where I go now for the awards, the medals, the parades and the commotion.

I grind my teeth to think of Germany and her infection of arrogance and weakness and cruelty that has spread to our own particular enemy, has set on foot this abominable war, has brought us all to this pass, and me to a hatred that is not without guilt, is not, is not a pure flame of altruism; ah, hatred is never this, is always rather to make use of this grand altruistic feeling, to bring to a head in ourselves all that there is in us of a hatred and fury upon a less convenient truth.

How apt I was for this deceit, how splendid a material, that recognizing the deceit must take commission under it, forever following darkness.

'Are you not interested in politics, in working for peace, in the fight against fascism?' said that young Professor Dryasdust to me back in England at our Edinburgh dinner-party.

'No, I am not interested to concentrate upon politics, fascism or communism, or upon any groupismus whatever; I am not interested to centre my thoughts in anything so frivolous as these variations upon a theme that is so banal, so boring, so bed-bottom false, so suspect in its origin. *C'est la vie entière que c'est mon métier.*' And the thoughts about the thoughts go round about in my head, to think of this so fascinating great field of exploration, that has for an adventure all of the mechanism of heresy, that the mind of a person must be for ever more interesting, more tantalizing to invite, than all of the thoughts it projects, that are but for a torchlight flame upon a part of it, to horrify perhaps, to please, but to invite.

C'est la vie entière que c'est mon métier. And jumping to my feet I cry aloud this sentence, that is so much more arrogant than all their arrogance, out-heroding the Herod of all their childish theories, that have in them so much a power for harm, so seeming-good, so honey-poisonous.

But how to be good, how quiet? It must be a personal orientation upon no human cause whatever. Not love, not love. I look at this dear Tom, so plaintively I look that he must smile.

'It's no good, Pompey, I cannot help you.'

He knows my thoughts, he is so sweet. Not love, not love. But I must kiss him now, he is so sweet.

'You lovely darling,' I say.

He laughs at this.

So now beneath the bearskin rug there is a little peace and quietness, enough to make a pocket handkerchief, enough for a pocket handkerchief, to blow away upon a puff of thought.

So now I am quiet and good. But love is a sort o sickness. So now I am quiet and good. But I am never good when I am well.

And has Tom found a quietness and a peace and a goodness that is something transcending the quietness, the peace and the goodness of a pussy-not-feel-well, of a love and an affection?

I cannot say, it is not something to talk about. And I turn in his arms again and cry out, it makes me almost cry to be so restless, so unquiet, so *farouche* and so boring for him.

I cry out, it is a poem I am trying to make up, it has for the last line to each verse, for a very rousing musical passage I have also in my head, that has not yet come to be completely exteriorized, that has these words for a line of poetry: O, circle of Trismegistus, oh where is your circumference?

I sing this aloud, to the notes of music that I have only so far succeeded to invent: and I jump up and down upon the bed, I feel so happy to be able to sing this to him, and he thinks that it will make a good poem, when the rest of it is arrived, having within it the germ of an idea of all of that something of a personal orientation about which I was talking.

And singing this over to Tom I am for the moment occupied with the idea of this musical passage, that must be something rousing and hymnlike, but not, dear Reader, hymnlike in the rather ridiculous bad Ancient and Modern hymnway.

Now when I was a young child at my first school, and in the kindergarten of this first school, we were allowed to choose our hymns, and also we were allowed to choose what songs we would like to sing in our singing class, that was taken by an aged gentle lady, with no thoughts upon discipline. That poor lady certainly had, by reason of this, a bad time of it, for as a group of child songsters we were up to no good, to not one good thing at all, but to crawl on the floor under the kindergarten tables, and swallow the bone gags we had each of us, to keep our mouths open, or rather to pretend to swallow them, and to choke and be sick, for the greater promotion of a general confusion.

Now I was telling Tom, lying beneath the bearskin rug, that the hymns we sang at this school were upon analysis a little peculiar for children to be singing.

Our headmistress was a serious-minded lady, of a liberal-socialistic turn of mind, and very much I admire her, for at this time, which was about 1914, she had the strength of her unpopular convictions, to stand up at that time and declare that war on the long view was not a good thing.

But she was very simple too, with not much of an idea of the humour of incongruity. So that well I remember the immensely humorous effect of one line of one of these hymns that said: 'Make one sad gigantic failure for eternity' but said it to so lilting and tripping a tune that even a baby must smile, and smile we did, or rather howl and roar, like the children of the devil that we were, that were too much for our singing mistress and our headmistress, that had somehow got a firm grip on the thought that child is but a synonym for sweetness and light.

So I was telling this to Tom, and singing gently to him all of these hymns that we used to sing in our kindergarten, and glad too that for many of these quiet nights we had a little of peace and quietness together again, that was set before upon a hateful enmity, and when it was twelve o'clock by the clock upon the wall, he was asleep, and the firelight was shining upon him softly.

So I must get up now, and standing over the bed I look down at his quiet face, that I must say good-bye to now, for a little time I must say good-bye to Tom. So I take off my dressing-gown and put on my uniform, that is not so hateful to me now at all, that drives away from my head at once all thoughts that are not thoughts about what I must now do. So I put on my uniform, and over it and reaching to the floor I lay my fur-lined cloak, that is so grand, so close-wrapped, so formidable, so complete. And I pull my cap down over my ears, and I have on my great riding boots. I pull on my gloves. So good-bye, dear Tom, good-bye. To-night I am to go to Mentz, riding alone through the dark night forests, along the snow-covered rides, and past the great ice-bound lakewater, with the dead branches of trees held fast in the ice-grip that is so cold, so cold and dead. And the reeds at the dark margin of the lakewater are silent now, no wind moves them. I know very well the way to go. Beau-Minon is saddled. It is past twelve o'clock.

From my conversations with Generalissimo and Archbishop two sentences stand out, to be remembered with some laughter and a little affront, for their context, so bewilderingly echt Mentz, for their content, so really horrifying.

I must give you my view of the Archbishop quickly now before I forget, for I am slipped back, the ground has slipped from under my conceited feet, I have slipped back into my former dream life of an imperfect outward consciousness.

I find the Archbishop violent, astute, unscrupulous and ridiculous in this, that he imagines me to be completely at one with him. Or is this only pretence, a movement of attack perhaps, in this dreamy maze, this heavy silent Approach-Recoil, that has in it the movements of a dance, a little difficult to follow, to see but one step at a time, to inveigle one's feet, past forgot, future unguessed, indifferently considered?

I am sitting in my room now, turning the pages of a brilliant picture-book the Archbishop has lent me. How lovely, how dark and brilliant these pages are, how entirely absorbing, how fascinating and how dangerous. For here are processions of kings and princes, great soldiers, conquerors, emperors – assassins. In pride and cruelty they possess the earth. How beautiful they are, how lovely, how forlorn. Ah for instance if they were only absurd, if I can only see that they are, in the exigeance of their pride, laughable, ridiculous, mice in motley, infinite in pretence, in value nothing.

But they do not appear to me to be so ridiculous at all; they are the flower of our humanity, the poison flower that is not less lovely for all its venom.

They turn and look at me, passing in military formation, in a pride of colour. Their faces are pale beneath a weight of gold, pale against crimson, scarlet, and a deeper red more deep than blood. I too have ridden in processions, have tasted the pride of privilege, have seen a throng of people in the streets, have felt the outrageous aloofness the cruelty the intolerance of a great position fittingly maintained. In the church where we went for our thanksgiving, it was a small church, very close with incense upon the air, with only space for our immediate train, there was hung behind the altar a great crucifixion picture in the manner of Grünewald. The body hangs forward from the cross, the head is bent forward, the thorns upon the crown drive the blood in streams upon the face, every muscle, every nerve and sinew, lives to endure a completion of pain, there is no ease in this body at all, there is no ease and no slackening of a consciousness. Ah is not this the quintessence of our invention that the God of our hope must suffer to be surveyed in a shameful death, to be worshipped so much only in the suffering he endured, his lineaments unknown except in torment? I move my head uneasily to see the Archbishop upon my right. This is the man, yes this is the man that said to me, that said this sentence I have not forgotten, sitting late last night with a benignity of condescension to discuss with me the process of the war, and its conclusion barely now within sight, but to be concluded upon a certain victory. 'Grief is not subject to the laws of the multiplication table.' Oh yes, so the death of 3000 men is no more, in its content of grief and attendant bereavement, than the death of one? And with this to salve our conscience we have a mandate. 'But yours is the prerogative of mercy.' 'Yes, mercy, – upon the longer view. The impulsive good of the moment is not always the ultimate and final good.'

Ah what is this cruel man thinking now, this ferocious old bore, what is he thinking, what tortuous thoughts to provide accustomed cover for a course that has his own advantage for a pointer to a hateful end?

I know now from whom I hold my commission, and I am sick with the weight of its fatality, but how escape, who have so much involved myself, too actively promoted his designs?

There is without me and around a force of false imagining, of vulgarity, of pride, of ostentation, no less inimical to me and no less vulgar than all of the hatred, pride of smugness and obstruction upon the eyes of the dying peasant. And within my heart are thoughts that thought for thought meet theirs, to bridge and fuse into a murderous intent.

I am not less guilty than peasant and Archbishop, not less guilty than frivolous and brilliant Generalissimo, with girlish lisp and frightful malice of intent upon the life of his father. This inspired tactician, this brilliant soldier, this parricide-in-posse.

No no, here I must laugh. I close my fascinating evil picture-book and walk about my room. For the Generalissimo said, in what honeyed accents of effete reproach, 'If only father would die, if only he would die, I'm sure he'd be happier dead.' And pausing, with needle lifted upon a square of petit-point, 'if only he were dead'.

I guess his father's life is not worth a great deal now, for there is also a current of ferocity in the voice of Clever-Pie, and if his father lets the reins of command fall lightly to his son, he keeps a heavy hand upon the coffers. And Clever-Pie will run him out by Christmas, I guess he will.

I like this little Clever-Pie. He is at least not so deadly boring as His Eminence.

And I remember another occasion. We were sitting in the evening at the table, over maps. And he said:

'What a girl you are for the glooms, my dear. I know these processions must be boring for you, after the refinements (an agreeable whinny) . . . the re-fi-hi-hinements of London. But once the old boy's gone, we'll cut out all that and clear up the war.'

'Do you think,' I ask, lifting an eyebrow at the Archbishop, comfortably a-doze in an armchair, 'do you think that he will *go* soon?'

'Oh him,' says Clever-Pie, 'I'm not thinking of him, I can manage him all right – interfering old cow.'

He also does not care so very much for the Archbishop, I see.

'It's father I'm thinking of.' (And he picks his nose in the most natural way possible.)

'By the way, Pompey, you're not nuts on Satterthwaite, are you, not going to do a bolt, eh? That would be a pity.'

'Why?'

'Why what? Oh, I see. Well for one thing, he's

not the man for you. You've got a sort of flair for all this, you know, quite remarkably strong, I find. Well, put up with the processions swings and roundabouts for a bit. After all, Daddy loves that sort of thing. And he won't be here long. *He won't be here long.*'

Oh how frightful this place is, and how beastly silly I have been, and is there now no remedy, am I too hopelessly involved, too set in and captive upon the will of these two men, upon my own pride, too satisfactory performance?

Round and round my room I walk. The heavy curtains hang against the walls, stirred by a little wind below the window sash. To-morrow we have a long programme of boring occasions, and more heavy feasting. But here the food is good. And the soup is hot, a thing we could never come at in our tower dwelling, so that always, for the delinquency of a shifty commissariat, I must say to Tom: Oh if only the soup were hot, oh if we could only have some hot soup, oh is there no hot soup to be had in this tower?

But here we feast well, and we jump about, and go in processions, and it is all so barbaric, so untimely, so out-of-time, so tedious. How could I, that was so clever, so much the clever Pompey that knew so much, how could I for one moment have thought to come here, to enjoy the processions, to be flattered by the attention of the Archbishop, the 'you're one of us, my dear' of the Generalissimo?

Again and again I wring my hands, I think: How hateful you are, Pompey, how appalling in a foolish ambition, how wrong-headed always in a wrong direction, how much of baseness there is in you, yes you are very base, I guess there is no hope in you, wedded to a vulgarity of absurd ambition, nourished upon a child's caudle of anger and impatience. And I am certain again that I have done something at which the crocodile must blench. Oh if only I could for once for instance do something at which the crocodile might keep his countenance.

But you see it is my fault I am in this galère, I have brought myself to this absurd pass. I may say I was shanghaied into this adventure, forced into a uniform I intuitively hated. But if there had been nothing in me of it, nothing to be called awake by this wretched event, should I not now be playing, in perhaps some boredom, but safely and sanely enough, with those who seem to me now beyond the frontier of a separate life?

I try the door of my room. It is locked on the outside. I had suspected as much. They are not so entirely certain of me. What use to call to death? What lies beyond? I might as well be dead, and in some place that is not heaven, what use to call to death? Or is corruption so certainly mortal? It is a foolish thought.

How restless I am. I try the window. That they could not lock upon the outside. Where have they stabled Beau-Minon? And if I ride off on my discovered horse, shall I not, returning at length to Tom, involve him also in some stricture, a penalty perhaps of life?

But no, I should have the night for my ride, and Mentz they will never leave, dare not, care not to, for neither the Archbishop nor the Generalissimo is an active campaigner, and will not care to have me sent for, would rather wait, could cut off our return if need be, standing between us and Tilssen.

Us? My dear Tom, I had told him in the end, how glad I am. I lay on his bed underneath the white bearskin.

'I am ordered to Mentz.'

'Careerist. Are you going?'

'Yes, I suppose so. Yes.'

'Yes, unqualified yes,' laughed Tom. 'Look here, my dear, watch your step. I don't say, Stay with me. If I did I was raving.'

'You were ill.'

'Well, put it like that. I don't say stay. If I were to

persuade you, I don't say for one moment mind you that I could, but if I did you would always imagine that you had missed something – well, rather not-to-be-missed. So run along and play with your Archbishop, your Generalissimo, your fur cloaks and brass bands . . . No I don't think it is a piece of vulgarity, for them it is not, it is perhaps a survival. Korda, shall we say, and Cecil B. de Mille have not spoilt it for them. And yet – very ferocious and astute animals they are for all their playacting. I must trust your common sense to make a getaway for you in time. Remember, the quality in you that Peck and I have found so quite invaluable may also appeal to them as something they can use, at short circuit, short circuiting me, that is. There is the least little bit of danger there, do you understand? So watch your step. And if you don't come back, be sure I shall come and fetch you. And when I come for you, you must be ready. Do you hear?' (he shakes me) 'You must be ready.'

'Ready for what?'

'Home.'

'Tilssen?'

'London.'

And now he is serious again and says: 'Watch your step. Pompey, be careful. For me this Mentz démarche would have little significance, for you – I don't know. We shall see what you will make of it.

And remember, Pompey, just this. You have involved yourself, oh so far very successfully, though I don't know that I should care to have that last success upon my conscience. But don't forget my dear, don't be too enthusiastic, you come fresh to the game, and I introduced you to it, so I too have my responsibility for what you do. Disinvolve yourself, if you can come to it, disinvolve, dissociate, hold a watching brief.'

Hold a watching brief. The fields of snow outside my window run up close to the palace wall, all is silent within and without, these men are cruel, ruthless, barbaric – but barbaric in a rococo rather amusing way. But am I not a little conceited to say I find them in fact, oh certainly not absurd, but rather amusing? For it might not be so very amusing for me, well suppose, if I did not do quite what they have in mind for me to do, that something that has not yet come out, to be made quite clear to me; but they are cruel and barbaric and ruthless to hold at all costs, at any cost whatever of pain and suffering to other people, the power of their privilege. Well, suppose. Again, is it not a familiar situation, with the things changed that must be changed. Are not all holders of privilege ruthless and cruel in their tenure, and if at home in London, in England, I have despised utterly and avoided the mentality that clings to privilege and the adroit vulgarity and stupidity that runs alongside, and here I do not, and here indeed I have allowed myself to be for a moment attracted, conceited to have the cloak of *their* privilege, for *their* purpose, thrown about my shoulders, is it not only because in modern times, in our London or New York of modern times, privilege is so familiar so obvious in its manière d'agir, so not-to-be-disguised, so appalling in its concomitants of envy hatred moonshine and baloney, so ridiculous in its certain outcroppings at every level of society? Privilege in sophistication must divest itself of the colour and integrity of performance I find here, must abhor the overt slap in the eye to humanistic ideology, the childish delight in a daily use of colour and form, the naïveté that has in it something of innocence.

But I have been mistaken. The spirit is the same, and now I recognize it very well for what it is, and in the vigour and barbaric splendour of its youth there is to be discerned the lineaments of a frightful maturity. Is then power and the lust for power the very stuff of our existence, the prop of our survival, our hope of the future, our despair of the past? And if we cannot achieve in our individualities this po wer are we any less guilty if we pursue it, or again, abandoning the sweet chase, identify ourselves with a national ethos, take pride in our country, in our country's plundering, or, if the mood takes us, in our country's victories upon other fields less barren, in science, art, jurisprudence, philosophy? Ours the privilege, to us the laurels. Oh corruption, of uncertain mortality, how divide, without a national death, the springs of our being, brought forth in pain and set to its infliction?

In the smug entertainment I found myself in the flattering incoherence of the Memoirs of Prince Von, so carefully excerpted, so many pages past, is there not this very frightfulness of an unsatisfied personal lust for power, identifying itself with a national arrogance, my country's successful delinquency? How base, despicable, how unutterably base. Have you no pride, no ambition? And are there no tears?

The thought and desire upon death is no salve for my mood, is but a cipher, an ignis fatuus, a foolish gesture, a child's scream of pain. Not self-violence upon the flesh, not a natural death, has promise of release. Power and cruelty are the strength of our life, and in its weakness only is there the sweetness of love.